MW00849309

"When I saw the first vers[...]
directed by Don Siegel, I [...]
contained more truth than any movie I had ever seen before."

Dean Koontz from his Introduction,
These Immigrants Don't Need No Stinkin' Green Cards!

"While the film is rightly credited with reflecting the anticommunist paranoia of the fifties, the novel's mood is different. It is more a cerebral science-fictional mystery."

Jon L. Breen from his essay, *The Fiction of Jack Finney*

"The gross-out level is one thing, but it is on that second level of horror that we often experience that low sense of anxiety which we call "the creeps." Over the years, *Invasion of the Body Snatchers* has given a lot of people the creeps."

Stephen King from his essay, *Invasion of the Body Snatchers*

"It's a classic—it'll be inscribed on my tombstone."

Kevin McCarthy on the original *Invasion of the Body Snatchers*

"I really didn't look on it as a remake. I looked on it as just another variation of the original theme... I would say that I was really more interested in the theme of paranoia, more of the Kafkaesque thing, which I felt was told really well both in the [1956] film and the Jack Finney book."

Philip Kaufman on the 1978 remake, *Invasion of the Body Snatchers*

"I wanted to do that film because the complexity of the source material transcends a particular zeitgeist of mid-fifties Americana. Like a lot of good science fiction, it's metaphor... It's a very scary movie, if I do say so myself."

Abel Ferrara on the 1997 remake, *Body Snatchers*

"I have read explanations of the 'meaning' of this story, which amuse me, because there is no meaning at all; it was just a story meant to entertain, and with no more meaning than that."

Jack Finney, author of *The Body Snatchers*

Dana Wynter, King Donovan, Carolyn Jones and Kevin McCarthy from Invasion of the Body Snatchers (1956)

INVASION OF THE BODY SNATCHERS: A TRIBUTE

Edited by Kevin McCarthy & Ed Gorman

STARK
HOUSE

Stark House Press • Eureka California

INVASION OF THE BODY SNATCHERS: A TRIBUTE

Published by Stark House Press
2200 O Street
Eureka, CA 95501, USA
griffinskye@cox.net
www.starkhousepress.com

ISBN: 1-9433586-07-9

Text set in Figural and Dogma. Heads set in Confidential.
Cover design and layout by Mark Shepard, shepdesign.home.comcast.net

PUBLISHER'S NOTE

First Stark House Press Edition: June 2006

0 9 8 7 6 5 4 3 2 1

TABLE OF CONTENTS

Introduction: These Immigrants Don't Need
No Stinkin' Green Cards! *Dean Koontz* 7

Invasion of the Body Snatchers *Stephen King* 13

The Fiction of Jack Finney *Jon L. Breen* 41

Of Time and Pods: The Fantastic World
of Jack Finney *Fred Blosser* 59

An Interview with Dana Wynter *Tom Weaver* 69

Philip Kaufman's Second Invasion *Tom Weaver* 94

An Interview with W. D. Richter *Matthew R. Bradley* 114

Robert H. Solo, Pod Producer *Anthony Timpone* 133

The Mark of Abel on a Classic:
An Interview with Abel Ferrara *Gilbert Colon* 160

The Unseen Body Snatchers *Anthony Timpone* 176

Will the Real Finale Please Take a Bow? *Tom Piccirilli* 197

Invasion of the Scene Stealers: My Second Career as a
Genre Icon *Kevin McCarthy as told to Matthew R. Bradley* . . . 203

Film Credits 234

Jack Finney Bibliography 237

INTRODUCTION: THESE IMMIGRANTS DON'T NEED NO STINKIN' GREEN CARDS!

— — —

Dean Koontz

When I saw the first version of *Invasion of the Body Snatchers,* directed by Don Siegel, I was only a kid, but I knew it contained more truth than any movie I had ever seen before.

I don't mean that I suddenly suspected the neighbors of having gone to high school in another galaxy or that I expected to find a giant pod tucked in the back of my closet. Well, okay, I *did* expect to find a giant pod in my closet, but the worst thing I ever turned up, after countless panicky searches night after night, was an old sneaker with an aromatic touch of mildew in it. And that was just last week.

When I say the movie brims with truth, I am not saying that the story line is literally true. Rather, it expresses profound truths through a compelling metaphor. Some critics have suggested that the film plays on fears of communism and is perhaps the most effective of the red-scare movies, but that's an inadequate interpretation. In the twentieth century, so *many* powerful forces have reshaped society so rapidly, compared to the more measured pace of change in previous centuries, that it's no surprise when we feel besieged and in danger of losing our humanity. Communism and fascism are the obvious examples of ideologies that not merely devalued the individual but denied legitimacy to the very idea that the masses exist for any purposes other than to serve an elite and to die for the philosophies of that elite. Yet an honest evaluation of most political movements that have followed the collapse of fascism and communism will reveal utopian fantasies of one stripe or another, each of which would sacrifice individuals to some imagined greater good and would result in hive societies that allow no freedom and no joy, except the psychotic joy of the true believer swept away by messianic rapture.

Even many basically nonpolitical movements with admirable intentions have embraced the antihuman attitudes and methodology of totalitarian ideologies. For example, though it is imperative that the environmental movement function rationally and successfully, if we are to have an ecologically healthy world to give to future generations, it seems as though half of the various organizations under the environmentalism umbrella have been co-opted by fanatics who want to use ecological concerns to effect social engineering that was tried and failed under both fascist and communist regimes; many actually argue that human beings are "unnatural," an infection that is destroying the planet, and that we have no right to be here.

The furious pace of technological change is another dehumanizing force. Labor-saving technology was supposed to give us more leisure time, but a greater percentage of our waking hours is spent in work or work-related tasks than ever before, as we spin like squirrels in exercise cages, desperate to keep current with change and, therefore, employable. This leaves less time for mothers and fathers to spend with their families and virtually no time at all to interact with their neighbors, to function as an integral part of their communities. A sense of isolation grows.

We were told that the information revolution would solve all the problems that previous technological change had wrought. The personal computer is indeed liberating, and the day may actually come when it saves us time rather than merely enabling us to do more work than ever before. Many claim to have found a sense of community through the Internet; but this can be little more than an illusion if few of these long-distance friendships result in the communicants meeting face-to-face and meaningfully interacting with one another beyond cyberspace. Relationship-building at a distance, through the filter of a computer, is ultimately ineffective for the sincere friend-seeker, but it is ideally suited to the sociopath whose powers of manipulation are enhanced when he can operate not merely behind his usual masks but behind an electronic mask as well. Many of us spend the evening hours online, staring at a screen rather than at human faces, communicating without the profound nuances of human voices and facial expressions, seeking sympathy and tenderness without the need to touch.

All the while, through our bones creeps the persistent feeling that we are losing our humanity. No wonder we *still* respond to Don Siegel's *Invasion of the Body Snatchers* so powerfully, even more than forty years after its initial release. Increasingly alienated from community, family, and friends, we feel an uneasiness that at times borders on paranoia.

When modern men and women lost religious faith, they lost the associated belief that human beings are special, that we were created with purpose to undertake a life with meaning. Science, technology, and politics have not yet filled that void and probably never will be able to do so, especially not if they continue to be powered by the ideologies that have thus far informed them. If we believe that we are just animals, without immortal souls, we are already but one step removed from pod people.

The original *Invasion of the Body Snatchers* has at its center this fundamental truth of modern life, which is why year by year its power as art grows rather than diminishes. Aware of how rarely the products of Hollywood contain any truth, I resisted seeing Philip Kaufman's—and W. D. Richter's—remake when it hit theaters. I assumed that it would not measure up to the original, that it would be packed with bogus and unnecessary special effects, that Hollywood once again would have succeeded in turning a silk purse into a sow's ear. When I finally watched it on laser disc, I was astonished and delighted to discover that it was a superb piece of work. By moving the setting from a small town to a metropolis, the director and screenwriter brought new power to the dual themes of alienation and dehumanization. The scenes near the end, in which packs of shadowy pod people rush through city streets in pursuit of the unconverted, bring instantly to mind images of Nazis chasing down Jews and evoke the terrors of every genocide, pogrom, and political repression that has made this such a century of shame.

I had thought that the inimitable Kevin McCarthy's superb, understated performance in the original couldn't be equaled. Although there is no entirely parallel role in the remake, Donald Sutherland's Matthew Bennell is as compelling as McCarthy's small-town doctor. The performances of Veronica Cartwright, Brooke Adams, and Jeff Goldblum help this version of the story to achieve immediacy and poignancy.

No films would have existed, of course, without Jack

Finney's classic science-fiction novel, *The Body Snatchers*. I have a long list of writers whose work I admire, and the reasons for admiring them are varied. I find Ray Bradbury's fiction exceptional because of his bold use of language, his willingness to take chances with wildly colorful metaphors and striking imagery, and his ebullience and contagious love of life. I can reread the best of James M. Cain, because his economical prose, his risky use of pulp conventions in a mainstream context, and his unblinking fascination with the dark side of the human heart are bracing. Few writers handle characterization, pace, and milieu a fraction as well as John D. MacDonald. I don't read Jack Finney for his style, which is clean and engaging but not as strongly personal as that of Bradbury. I don't read Finney for his narrative pace, which is compelling enough but which is certainly not marked by breathless suspense. To me, one of the greatest strengths of Jack Finney's work is his ability to describe and explore complex emotions in an admirably low-key fashion that nevertheless leaves the reader saying, "Yes, I know exactly how that feels." This is a considerable achievement. Dickens could do it. Comparatively few are good at it. Even writers whose novels scintillate with ideas, atmosphere, and mood are often emotionally dead on the page. In some, this may result from inadequate empathy; others may produce emotionally barren work because they mistakenly equate genuine sentiment with sentimentality and fear being pilloried by sarcastic critics. Finney's two most famous novels—*The Body Snatchers* and *Time and Again*—make us *feel*, and that is why they have such lasting power, though each tale evokes a rather different set of emotions. This is also why Finney's work is well suited to film adaptation: film is fundamentally an emotional rather than intellectual medium. Which is not to say that Finney's books lack intellectual content; indeed, we feel

what these characters feel precisely because they are people who *think,* people of some charm and wit. Fear, joy,
loneliness, longing—Finney had a way with this material,
and that was a gift of gold to Don Siegel, Daniel Mainwaring, Philip Kaufman, and W. D. Richter.

It's a gift of gold to all of us, in fact, and tonight I'm going
to treat myself to a double feature: the Siegel and Kaufman
versions. First, of course, I'll inspect the back of my closet.
And look under the bed. And see if there's anything odd in
the garage cabinets. I ought to do a quick search of the
attic, too, and make sure there's nothing but a spare tire in
the trunk of the car. And, hey, with all the companies dealing in house alarms and personal-security these days, why
hasn't *someone* invented a device that can warn you if the
person to whom you're talking is composed of a significant
percentage of vegetable matter? We really *need* a gadget
like that. We really, really do.

INVASION OF THE BODY SNATCHERS

— — —

Stephen King

Let me suggest that one of the films of the last thirty years to find a pressure point with great accuracy was Don Siegel's *Invasion of the Body Snatchers*. Further along, we'll discuss the novel—and Jack Finney, the author, will also have a few things to say—but for now, let's look briefly at the film.

There is nothing really physically horrible in the Siegel version of *Invasion of the Body Snatchers;** no gnarled and evil star travelers here, no twisted, mutated shape under the facade of normality. The pod people are just a little different, that's all. A little vague. A little messy. Although Finney never puts this fine a point on it in his book, he certainly suggests that the most horrible thing about "them" is that they lack even the most common and easily attainable sense of aesthetics. Never mind, Finney suggests,

---

*There is in the Philip Kaufman remake, though. There is a moment in that film which is repulsively horrible. It comes when Donald Sutherland uses a rake to smash in the face of a mostly formed pod. This "person's" face breaks in with sickening ease, like a rotted piece of fruit, and lets out an explosion of the most realistic stage blood that I have ever seen in a color film. When that moment came, I winced, clapped a hand over my mouth... and wondered how in the hell the movie had ever gotten its PG rating.

that these usurping aliens from outer space can't appreciate
La Traviata or *Moby Dick* or even a good Norman Rockwell
cover on the *Saturday Evening Post*. That's bad enough,
but—my God!—they don't mow their lawns or replace the
pane of garage glass that got broken when the kid down
the street batted a baseball through it. They don't repaint
their houses when they get flaky. The roads leading into
Santa Mira, we're told, are so full of potholes and washouts
that pretty soon the salesmen who service the town—who
aerate its municipal lungs with the life-giving atmosphere
of capitalism, you might say—will no longer bother to
come.

The gross-out level is one thing, but it is on that second
level of horror that we often experience that low sense of
anxiety which we call "the creeps." Over the years, *Invasion
of the Body Snatchers* has given a lot of people the creeps,
and all sorts of high-flown ideas have been imputed to
Siegel's film version. It was seen as an anti-McCarthy film
until someone pointed out the fact that Don Siegel's political views could hardly be called leftish. Then people began
seeing it as a "better dead than Red" picture. Of the two
ideas, I think that second one better fits the film that Siegel
made, the picture that ends with Kevin McCarthy in the
middle of a freeway, screaming "They're here already!
You're next!" to cars which rush heedlessly by him. But in
my heart, I don't really believe that Siegel was wearing a
political hat at all when he made the movie (and you will
see later that Jack Finney has never believed it, either); I
believe he was simply having fun and that the under-
tones... just happened.

This doesn't invalidate the idea that there is an allegorical
element in *Invasion of the Body Snatchers;* it is simply to suggest that sometimes these pressure points, these terminals
of fear, are so deeply buried and yet so vital that we may

Dana Wynter and Kevin McCarthy in a scene
from Invasion of the Body Snatchers (1956)

tap them like artesian wells—saying one thing out loud while we express something else in a whisper. The Philip Kaufman version of Finney's novel is fun (although, to be fair, not quite as much fun as Siegel's), but that whisper has changed into something entirely different: the subtext of Kaufman's picture seems to satirize the whole I'm-okay-you're-okay-so-let's-get-in-the-hot-tub-and-massage-our-precious-consciousness movement of the egocentric seventies. Which is to suggest that, although the uneasy dreams of the mass subconscious may change from decade to decade, the pipeline into that well of dreams remains constant and vital.

This is the real danse macabre, I suspect: those remarkable moments when the creator of a horror story is able to unite the conscious and subconscious mind with one potent idea. I believe it happened to a greater degree with the Siegel version of *Invasion of the Body Snatchers,* but of course both Siegel and Kaufman were able to proceed courtesy of Jack Finney, who sank the original well.

From urban paranoia to small-town paranoia: Jack Finney's *The Body Snatchers.** Finney himself has the following things to say about his book, which was originally published as a Dell paperback original in 1955:

"The book... was written in the early 1950s, and I don't really remember a lot about it. I do recall that I simply felt in the mood to write something about a strange event or a series of them in a small town; something inexplicable.

---

*As previously noted, the late-seventies remake of the Finney novel resets the story in San Francisco, opting for an urban paranoia which results in a number of sequences strikingly like those which open Polanski's film version of *Rosemary's Baby.* But Philip Kaufman lost more than he gained, I think, by taking Finney's story out of its natural small-town-with-a-handstand-in-the-park setting.

And that my first thought was that a dog would be injured or killed by a car, and it would be discovered that a part of the animal's skeleton was of stainless steel; bone and steel intermingled, that is, a thread of steel running into bone and bone into steel so that it was clear the two had grown together. But this idea led to nothing in my mind.... I remember that I wrote the first chapter—pretty much as it appeared, if I am recalling correctly—in which people complained that someone close to them was in actuality an imposter. But I didn't know where this was to lead, either. However, during the course of fooling around with this, trying to make it work out, I came across a reputable scientific theory that objects might in fact be pushed through space by the pressure of light, and that dormant life of some sort might conceivably drift through space... and [this] eventually worked the book out.

"I was never satisfied with my own explanation of how these dry leaflike objects came to resemble the people they imitated; it seemed, and seems, weak, but it was the best I could do.

"I have read explanations of the 'meaning' of this story, which amuse me, because there is no meaning at all; it was just a story meant to entertain, and with no more meaning than that. The first movie version of the book followed the book with great faithfulness, except for the foolish ending; and I've always been amused by the contentions of people connected with the picture that they had a message of some sort in mind. If so, it's a lot more than I ever did, and since they followed my story very closely, it's hard to see how this message crept in. And when the message has been defined, it has always sounded a little simple-minded to me. The idea of writing a whole book in order to say that it's not really a good thing for us all to be alike, and that individuality is a good thing, makes me laugh."

Nevertheless, Jack Finney has written a great deal of fiction about the idea that individuality is a good thing and that conformity can start to get pretty scary after it passes a certain point.

His comments (in a letter to me dated December 24, 1979) about the first film version of *The Body Snatchers* raised a grin on my own face as well. As Pauline Kael, Penelope Gilliatt, and all of those sober-sided film critics so often prove, no one is so humorless as a big-time film critic or so apt to read deep meanings into simple doings ("In *The Fury,*" Pauline Kael intoned, apparently in all seriousness, "Brian De Palma has found the junk heart of America.")—it is as if these critics feel it necessary to prove and re-prove their own literacy; they are like teenage boys who feel obliged to demonstrate and redemonstrate their macho... perhaps most of all to themselves. This may be because they are working on the fringes of a field which deals entirely with pictures and the spoken word; they must surely be aware that while it requires at least a high-school education to understand and appreciate all the facets of even such an accessible book as *The Body Snatchers,* any illiterate with four dollars in his or her pocket can go to a movie and find the junk heart of America. Movies are merely picture books that talk, and this seems to have left many literate movie critics with acute feelings of inferiority. Filmmakers themselves are often happy to participate in this grotesque critical overkill, and I applauded Sam Peckinpah in my heart when he made this laconic reply to a critic who asked him why he had *really* made such a violent picture as *The Wild Bunch:* "I like shoot-em-ups." Or so he was reputed to have said, and if it ain't true, gang, it oughtta be.

The Don Siegel version of *The Body Snatchers* is an amusing case where the film critics tried to have it both ways.

They began by saying that both Finney's novel and Siegel's film were allegories about the witch-hunt atmosphere that accompanied the McCarthy hearings. Then Siegel himself spoke up and said that this film was really about the Red Menace. He did not go so far as to say that there was a Commie under every American's bed, but there can be little doubt that Siegel at least believed he was making a movie about a creeping fifth column. It is the ultimate in paranoia, we might say: they're out there *and they look just like us!*

In the end it's Finney who comes away sounding the most right; *The Body Snatchers* is just a good story, one to be read and savored for its own unique satisfactions. In the quarter-century since its original publication as a humble paperback original (a shorter version appeared in *Collier's,* one of those good old magazines that fell by the wayside in order to make space on the newsstands of America for such intellectual publications as *Hustler, Screw,* and *Big Butts),* the book has been rarely out of print. It reached its nadir as a Fotonovel in the wake of the Philip Kaufman remake; if there is a lower, slimier, more antibook concept than the Fotonovel, I don't know what it would be. I think I'd rather see my kids reading a stack of Beeline Books than one of those photo-comics.

It reached its zenith as a Gregg Press hardcover in 1976. Gregg Press is a small company which has re-issued some fifty or sixty science fiction and fantasy books—novels, collections, and anthologies—originally published as paperbacks, in hardcover. The editors of the Gregg series (David Hartwell and L. W. Currey) have chosen wisely and well, and in the library of any reader who cares honestly about science fiction—and about books themselves as lovely artifacts—you're apt to find one or more of these distinctive green volumes with the red-gold stamping on the spines.

Oh dear God, we're off on another tangent. Well, never mind; I believe that what I started to say was simply that I think Finney's contention that *The Body Snatchers* is just a story is both right and wrong. My own belief about fiction, long and deeply held, is that story *must* be paramount over all other considerations in fiction; that story *defines* fiction, and that all other considerations—theme, mood, tone, symbol, style, even characterization—are expendable. There are critics who take the strongest possible exception to this view of fiction, and I really believe that they are the critics who would feel vastly more comfortable if *Moby Dick* were a doctoral thesis on cetology rather than an account of what happened on the *Pequod's* final voyage. A doctoral thesis is what a million student papers have reduced this tale to, but the story still remains—"This is what happened to Ishmael." As story still remains in *Macbeth, The Faerie Queen, Pride and Prejudice, Jude the Obscure, The Great Gatsby...* and Jack Finney's *The Body Snatchers*. And story, thank God, after a certain point becomes irreducible, mysterious, impervious to analysis. You will find no English master's thesis in any college library titled "The Story-Elements of Melville's *Moby Dick.*" And if you do find such a thesis, send it to me. I'll eat it. With A-1 Steak Sauce.

All very fine. And yet I don't think Finney would argue with the idea that story values are determined by the mind through which they are filtered, and that the mind of any writer is a product of his outer world and inner temper. It is just the fact of this filter that has set the table for all those would-be English M.A.'s, and I certainly would not want you to think that I begrudge them their degrees— God knows that as an English major I slung enough bullshit to fertilize most of east Texas—but a great number of the people who are sitting at the long and groaning table of Graduate Studies in English are cutting a lot of invisible steaks and roasts... not to mention trading the Emperor's new clothes briskly back and forth in what may be the largest academic yard sale the world has ever seen.

Still, what we have here is a Jack Finney novel, and we can say certain things about it simply because it is a Jack Finney novel. First, we can say that it will be grounded in absolute reality—a prosy reality that is almost humdrum, at least to begin with. When we first meet the book's hero (and here I think Finney probably would object if I used the more formal word *protagonist*... so I won't), Dr. Miles Bennell, he is letting his last patient of the day out; a sprained thumb. Becky Driscoll enters—and how is that for the perfect all-American name?—with the first off-key note: her cousin Wilma has somehow gotten the idea that her uncle Ira really isn't her uncle anymore. But this note is faint and barely audible under the simple melodies of small-town life that Finney plays so well in the book's opening chapters... and Finney's rendering of the small-town archetype in this book may be the best to come out of the 1950s.

The keynote that Finney sounds again and again in these first few chapters is so low-key pleasant that in less sure hands it would become insipid: nice. Again and again Finney returns to that word; things in Santa Mira, he tells us, are not great, not wild and crazy, not terrible, not boring. Things in Santa Mira are nice. No one here is laboring under that old Chinese curse "May you live in interesting times."

"For the first time I really saw her face again. I saw it was the same nice face..." This from page nine. A few pages later: "It was nice out, temperature around sixty-five, and the light was good;... still plenty of sun."

Cousin Wilma is also nice, if rather plain. Miles thinks she would have made a good wife and mother, but she just never married. "That's how it goes," Miles philosophizes, innocently unaware of any banality. He tells us he wouldn't have believed her the type of woman to have mental problems, "but still, you never know."

This stuff shouldn't work, and yet somehow it does; we feel that Miles has somehow stepped through the first-person convention and is actually talking to us, just as it seems that Tom Sawyer is actually talking to us in the Twain novel... and Santa Mira, California, as Finney presents it to us, is exactly the sort of town where we would almost expect to see Tom whitewashing a fence (there would be no Huck around, sleeping in a hogshead, though; not in Santa Mira).

The Body Snatchers is the only Finney book which can rightly be called a horror novel, but Santa Mira—which is a typical "nice" Finney setting—is the perfect locale for such a tale. Perhaps one horror novel is all that Finney had to write; certainly it was enough to set the mold for what we now call "the modern horror novel." If there is such a thing, there can be no doubt at all that Finney had a large hand in inventing it. I have used the phrase "off-key note" earlier on, and that is Finney's actual method in *The Body Snatchers,* I think; one off-key note, then two, then a ripple, then a run of them. Finally the jagged, discordant music of horror overwhelms the melody entirely. But Finney understands that there is no horror without beauty; no discord without a prior sense of melody; no nasty without nice.

There are no Plains of Leng here; no Cyclopean ruins under the earth; no shambling monsters in the subway tunnels under New York. At about the same time Jack Finney was writing *The Body Snatchers,* Richard Matheson was writing his classic short story "Born of Man and Woman," the story that begins: "today my mother called me retch. you retch she said." Between the two of them, they made the break from the Lovecraftian fantasy that had held sway over serious American writers of horror for two decades or more. Matheson's short story was published well before *Weird Tales* went broke; Finney's novel was published by Dell a year after. Although Matheson published two early short stories in *Weird Tales,* neither writer is associated with this icon of American fantasy-horror magazines; they represent the birth of an almost entirely new breed of American fantasist, just as, in the years 1977-1980, the emergence of Ramsey Campbell and Robert Aickman in England may represent another significant turn of the wheel.*

I have mentioned that Finney's short story "The Third Level" predates Rod Serling's *The Twilight Zone* series; in exactly the same fashion, Finney's little town of Santa Mira predates and points the way toward Peter Straub's fictional town of Milburn, New York; Thomas Tryon's Cornwall Coombe, Connecticut; and my own little town of Salem's Lot, Maine. It is even possible to see Finney's influence in Blatty's *The Exorcist,* where foul doings become fouler when set against the backdrop of Georgetown, a suburb which is quiet, graciously rich... and nice.

Finney concentrates on sewing a seam between the prosaic reality of his little you-can-see-it-before-your-eyes town and the outright fantasy of the pods which will follow. He sews the seam with such fine stitchwork that when we cross over from the world that really is and into a

---

*At the same time Finney and Matheson began administering their own particular brands of shock treatment to the American imagination, Ray Bradbury began to be noticed in the fantasy community, and during the fifties and sixties, Bradbury's name would become the one most readily identified with the genre in the mind of the general reading public. But for me, Bradbury lives and works alone in his own country, and his remarkable, iconoclastic style has never been successfully imitated. Vulgarly put, when God made Ray Bradbury He broke the mold.

world of utter make-believe, we are hardly aware of any
change. This is a major feat, and like the magician who can
make the cards walk effortlessly over the tips of his fingers
in apparent defiance of gravity, it looks so easy that you'd
be tempted to believe anyone could do it. You see the trick,
but not the long hours of practice that went into creating
the effect.

We have spoken briefly of paranoia in *Rosemary's Baby;* in
The Body Snatchers, the paranoia becomes full, rounded, and
complete. If we are all incipient paranoids—if we all take a
quick glance down at ourselves when laughter erupts at
the cocktail party, just to make sure we're zipped up and it
isn't us they're laughing at—then I'd suggest that Finney
uses this incipient paranoia quite deliberately to manipu-
late our emotions in favor of Miles, Becky, and Miles's
friends, the Belicecs.

Wilma, for instance, can present no proof that her uncle
Ira is no longer her uncle Ira, but she impresses us with
her strong conviction and with a deep, free-floating anxiety as pervasive as a migraine headache. Here is a kind of
paranoid dream, as seamless and as perfect as anything out
of a Paul Bowles novel or a Joyce Carol Oates tale of the
uncanny:

*Wilma sat staring at me, eyes intense. "I've been waiting for
today," she whispered. "Waiting till he'd get a haircut, and he
finally did." Again she leaned toward me, eyes big, her voice a
hissing whisper. "There's a little scar on the back of Ira's neck; he
had a boil there once, and your father lanced it. You can't see the
scar," she whispered, "when he needs a haircut. But when his
neck is shaved, you can. Well, today—I've been waiting for
this!—today he got a haircut—"*

*I sat forward, suddenly excited. "And the scar's gone? You
mean—"*

*"No!" she said, almost indignantly, eyes flashing. "It's there—
the scar—exactly like Uncle Ira's!"*

So Finney serves notice that we are working here in a
world of utter subjectivity... and utter paranoia. Of course
we believe Wilma at once, even though we have no real
proof; if for no other reason, we know from the title of the
book that the "body snatchers" are out there somewhere.
By putting us on Wilma's side from the start, Finney has
turned us into equivalents of John the Baptist, crying in
the wilderness. It is easy enough to see why the book was
eagerly seized upon by those who felt, in the early fifties,
that there was either a communist conspiracy afoot, or perhaps a fascist conspiracy that was operating in the name of
anti-communism. Because, either way or neither way, this
is a book about conspiracy with strong paranoid over-
tones... in other words, exactly the sort of story to be
claimed as political allegory by political loonies of every
stripe.

Earlier on, I mentioned the idea that perfect paranoia is
perfect awareness. To that we could add that paranoia may
be the last defense of the overstrained mind. Much of the
literature of the twentieth century, from such diverse
sources as Bertolt Brecht, Jean-Paul Sartre, Edward Albee,
Thomas Hardy, even F. Scott Fitzgerald, has suggested that
we live in an existential sort of world, a planless insane
asylum where things just happen. IS GOD DEAD? asks the
Time magazine cover in the waiting room of Rosemary
Woodhouse's Satanic obstetrician. In such a world it is perfectly credible that a mental defective should sit on the
upper floor of a little-used building, wearing a Hanes T-
shirt, eating take-out chicken, and waiting to use his mail-
order rifle to blow out the brains of an American president;
perfectly possible that another mental defective should be

able to stand around in a hotel kitchen a few years later
waiting to do exactly the same thing to that defunct president's younger brother; perfectly understandable that nice
American boys from Iowa and California and Delaware
should have spent their tours in Vietnam collecting ears,
many of them extremely tiny; that the world should begin
to move once more toward the brink of an apocalyptic war
because of the preachings of an eighty-year-old Moslem
holy man who is probably foggy on what he had for breakfast by the time sunset rolls around.

All of these things are mentally acceptable if we accept
the idea that God has abdicated for a long vacation, or has
perchance really expired. They are mentally acceptable, but
our emotions, our spirits, and most of all our passion for
order—these powerful elements of our human makeup—
all rebel. If we suggest that there was no reason for the
deaths of six million Jews in the camps during World War
II, no reason for poets bludgeoned, old women raped, children turned into soap, that it just happened and nobody
was really responsible—things just got a little out of control here, ha-ha, so sorry—then the mind begins to totter.

I saw this happen at first-hand in the sixties, at the
height of the generational shudder that began with our
involvement in Vietnam and went on to encompass everything from parietal hours on college campuses and the vot-
ing franchise at eighteen to corporate responsibility for
environmental pollution.

I was in college at the time, attending the University of
Maine, and while I began college with political leanings
too far to the right to actually become radicalized, by 1968
my mind had been changed forever about a number of fundamental questions. The hero of Jack Finney's later novel,
Time and Again, says it better than I could:

"I was... an ordinary person who long after he was grown retained the childhood assumption that the people who largely control our lives are somehow better informed than, and have judgment superior to, the rest of us; that they are more intelligent. Not until Vietnam did I finally realize that some of the most important decisions of all time can be made by men knowing really no more than most of the rest of us."

For me, it was a nearly overwhelming discovery—one that really began to happen, perhaps, on that day in the Stratford Theater when the announcement that the Russians had orbited a space satellite was made to me and my contemporaries by a theater manager who looked like he had been gutshot at close range.

But for all of that, I found it impossible to embrace the mushrooming paranoia of the last four years of the sixties completely. In 1968, during my junior year at college, three Black Panthers from Boston came to my school and talked (under the auspices of the Public Lecture Series) about how the American business establishment, mostly under the guidance of the Rockefellers and AT&T, was responsible for creating the neofascist political state of Amerika, encouraging the war in Vietnam because it was good for business, and also encouraging an ever more virulent climate of racism, stateism, and sexism. Johnson was their puppet; Humphrey and Nixon were also their puppets; it was a case of "meet the new boss, same as the old boss," as the Who would say a year or two later; the only solution was to take it into the streets. They finished with the Panther slogan, "All power comes out of the barrel of a gun," and adjured us to remember Fred Hampton.

Now, I did not and do not believe that the hands of the Rockefellers were utterly clean during that period, nor those of AT&T; I did and do believe that companies like

Sikorsky and Douglas Aircraft and Dow Chemical and even
the Bank of America subscribed more or less to the idea
that war is good business (but never invest your son as
long as you can slug the draft board in favor of the right
kind of people; when at all possible, feed the war machine
the spics and the niggers and the poor white trash from
Appalachia, but not our boys, oh no, never *our* boys!); I did
and do believe that the death of Fred Hampton was a case
of police manslaughter at the very least. But these Black
Panthers were suggesting a huge umbrella of conscious
conspiracy that was laughable... except the audience wasn't
laughing. During the Q-and-A period, they were asking
sober, concerned questions about just how the conspiracy
was working, who was in charge, how they got their orders
out, et cetera.

Finally I got up and said something like, "Are you really
suggesting that there is an actual Board of Fascist Conspiracy in this country? That the conspirators—the presidents
of GM and Esso, plus David and Nelson Rockefeller—are
maybe meeting in a big underground chamber beneath the
Bonneville Salt Flats with agendas containing items on
how more blacks can be drafted and the war in Southeast
Asia prolonged?" I was finishing with the suggestion that
perhaps these executives were arriving at their underground fortress in flying saucers—thus handily accounting
for the upswing in UFO sightings as well as for the war in
Vietnam—when the audience began to shout angrily for
me to sit down and shut up. Which I did posthaste, blush-
ing furiously, knowing how those eccentrics who mount
their soapboxes in Hyde Park on Sunday afternoons must
feel. I did not much relish the feeling.

The Panther who spoke did not respond to my question
(which, to be fair, wasn't a question at all, really); he merely said softly, "*You* got a surprise, didn't you, man?" This

was greeted with a burst of applause and laughter from the audience.

I *did* get a surprise—and a pretty unpleasant one, at that. But some thought has convinced me that it was impossible for those of my generation, propelled harum-scarum through the sixties, hair flying back from our foreheads, eyes bugging out with a mixture of delight and terror, from the Kingsmen doing "Louie Louie" to the blasting fuzztones of the Jefferson Airplane, to get from point A to point Z without a belief that someone—even Nelson Rockefeller— was pulling the strings.

In various ways throughout this book I've tried to suggest that the horror story is in many ways an optimistic, upbeat experience; that it is often the tough mind's way of coping with terrible problems which may not be supernatural at all but perfectly real. Paranoia may be the last and strongest bastion of such an optimistic view—it is the mind crying out, "*Something* rational and understandable is going on here! These things *do not just happen!*"

So we look at a shadow and say there was a man on the grassy knoll at Dallas; we say that James Earl Ray was in the pay of certain big Southern business interests, or maybe the CIA; we ignore the fact that American business interests exist in complex circles of power, often revolving in direct opposition to one another, and suggest that our stupid but mostly well-meant involvement in Vietnam was a conspiracy hatched by the military-industrial complex; or that, as a recent rash of badly spelled and printed posters in New York suggested, that the Ayatollah Khomeini is a puppet of—yeah, you guessed it—David Rockefeller. We suggest, in our endless inventiveness, that Captain Mantell did not die of oxygen starvation back there in 1947 while chasing that odd daytime reflection of Venus which veteran pilots call a sundog; no, he was chasing a ship from another world which exploded his plane with a death ray when he got too close.

It would be wrong of me to leave you with any impression that I am inviting the two of us to have a good laugh at these things together; I am not. These things are not the beliefs of madmen but the beliefs of sane men and women trying desperately, not to preserve the status quo, but just to find the fucking thing. And when Becky Driscoll's cousin Wilma says her uncle Ira isn't her uncle Ira, we believe her instinctively and immediately. If we don't believe her, all we've got is a spinster going quietly dotty in a small California town. The idea does not appeal; in a sane world, nice middle-aged ladies like Wilma aren't s'posed to go bonkers. It isn't right. There's a whisper of chaos in it that's somehow more scary than believing she might be right about Uncle Ira. We believe because belief affirms the lady's sanity. We believe her because... because... *because something is going on!* All those paranoid fantasies are really not fantasies at all. We—and Cousin Wilma— are right; it's the *world* that's gone haywire. The idea that the world has gone haywire is pretty bad, but as we can cope with Bill Nolan's fifty-foot bug once we see what it really is, so we can cope with a haywire world if we just know where our feet are planted. Bob Dylan speaks to the existentialist in us when he tells us that "Something is going on here/But you don't know what it is/Do you, Mr. Jones?" Finney—in the guise of Miles Bennell—takes us firmly by the arm and tells us that he knows exactly what's going on here: it's those goddamn pods from space! *They're* responsible!

It's fun to trace the classic threads of paranoia Finney weaves into his story. While Miles and Becky are at a movie, Miles's writer friend Jack Belicec asks Miles to come and take a look at something he's found in his basement.

The something turns out to be the body of a naked man on a pool table, a body which seems to Miles, Becky, Jack, and Jack's wife, Theodora, somehow unformed—not yet quite shaped. It's a pod, of course, and the shape it is taking is Jack's own. Shortly we have concrete proof that something is terribly wrong:

Becky actually moaned when we saw the [finger] prints, and I think we all felt sick. Because it's one thing to speculate about a body that's never been alive, a blank. But it's something very different, something that touches whatever is primitive deep in your brain, to have that speculation proved. There were no prints; there were five absolutely smooth, solidly black circles.

These four—now aware of the pod conspiracy—agree not to call the police immediately but to see how the pods develop. Miles takes Becky home and then goes home himself, leaving the Belicecs to stand watch over the thing on the pool table. But in the middle of the night Theodora Belicec freaks out and the two of them show up on Miles's doorstep. Miles calls a psychiatrist friend, Mannie Kaufman (a shrink? we are immediately suspicious; we don't need a shrink here, we want to shout at Miles; call out the army!), to come and sit with the Belicecs while he goes after Becky... who earlier has confessed to feeling that her father is no longer her father.

On the bottom shelf of a cupboard in the Driscoll basement, Miles finds a blank which is developing into a pseudo-Becky. Finney does a brilliant job of describing what this coming-to-being would look like. He compares it to fine-stamping medallions; to developing a photograph; and later to those eerie, lifelike South American dolls. But in our current state of high nervousness, what really impresses us is how neatly the thing has been tucked away, hidden behind a closed door in a dusty basement, biding its time.

Becky has been drugged by her "father," and in a scene simply charged with romance, Miles spirits her out of the house and carries her through the sleeping streets of Santa Mira in his arms; it is no trick to imagine the gauzy stuff of her nightgown nearly glowing in the moonlight.

And the fallout of all this? When Mannie Kaufman arrives, the men return to the Belicec house to investigate the basement:

There was no body on the table. Under the bright, shadowless light from the overhead lay the brilliant green felt, and on the felt, except at the corners and along the sides, lay a sort of thick gray fluff that might have fallen, or been jarred loose, I supposed, from the open rafters.

For an instant, his mouth hanging open, Jack stared at the table. Then he swung to Mannie, and his voice protesting, asking for belief; he said, "It was there on the table! Mannie, it was!"

Mannie smiled, nodding quickly. "I believe you, Jack..."

But we know that's what all of these shrinks say... just before they call for the men in the white coats. We know that fluff isn't just fluff from the overhead rafters; the damned thing has gone to seed. But nobody else knows it, and Jack is quickly reduced to the final plea of the helpless paranoiac: You gotta believe me, doc!

Mannie Kaufman's rationalization for the increasing number of people in Santa Mira who no longer believe their relatives are their relatives is that Santa Mirans are undergoing a case of low-key mass hysteria, the sort of thing that may have been behind the Salem witch trials, the mass suicides in Guyana, even the dancing sickness of the middle ages. But below this rationalistic approach, existentialism lurks unpleasantly. These things happen, he seems to suggest, just because they happen. Sooner or later they will work themselves out.

They do, too. Mrs. Seeley, who believed her husband wasn't her husband, comes in to tell Miles that everything is fine now. Ditto the girls who were scared of their English instructor for a while. And ditto Cousin Wilma, who calls up Miles to tell him how embarrassed she is at having caused such a fuss; of *course* Uncle Ira is Uncle Ira. And in every case, one other fact—a name—stands out: Mannie Kaufman was there, helping them all. Something is wrong here, all right, but we know very well what it is, thank you, Mr. Jones. We have noticed the way Kaufman's name keeps cropping up. We're not stupid, right? Damn right we're not! And it's pretty obvious that Mannie Kaufman is now playing for the visiting team.

And one more thing. At Jack Belicec's insistence, Miles finally decides to call a friend in the Pentagon and spill the whole incredible story. About his long distance call to Washington, Miles tells us:

It isn't easy explaining a long, complicated story over the telephone …And we had bad luck with the connection. At first I heard Ben and he heard me, as clearly as though we were next door to each other. But when I began telling him what had been happening here, the connection faded. Ben had to keep asking me to repeat, and I almost had to shout to make him understand me. You can't talk well, you can't even think properly, when you have to repeat every other phrase, and I signaled the operator and asked for a better connection… I'd hardly resumed when a sort of buzzing sound started in the receiver in my ear, and then I had to try to talk over that…

"They," of course, are now in charge of communications coming into and going out of Santa Mira ("We are controlling transmission," that somehow frightening voice which introduced *The Outer Limits* each week used to say; "*We* will control the horizontal... *we* will control the vertical... we can roll the image, make it flutter... we can change the focus..."). Such a passage will also strike a responsive chord in any old antiwar protester, SDS member, or activist who ever believed his or her home phone was tapped or that the guy with the Nikon on the edge of the demonstration was taking his or her picture for a dossier someplace. *They* are everywhere; *they* are watching; *they* are listening. Surely it is no wonder that Siegel believed that Finney's novel was about a-Red-under-every-bed or that others believed it was about the creeping fascist menace. As we descend deeper and deeper into the whirlpool of this nightmare it might even become possible to believe it was the pod people who were on the grassy knoll in Dallas, or that it was the pod people who obediently swallowed their poisoned Kool-Aid at Jonestown and then spritzed it down the throats of their squalling infants. It would be such a relief to be able to believe that.

Miles's conversation with his army friend is the book's clearest delineation of the paranoid mind at work. Even when you know the whole story, you aren't allowed to communicate it to those in authority... and it's hard to think with that buzzing in your head!

Linked to this is the strong sense of xenophobia Finney's major characters feel. The pods really are "a threat to our way of life," as Joe McCarthy used to say. "They'll have to declare martial law," Jack tells Miles, "a state of siege, or something—anything! And then do whatever has to be done. Root this thing out, smash it, crush it, kill it."

Later, during their brief flight from Santa Mira, Miles and Jack discover two pods in the trunk of the car. This is how Miles describes what happens next:

And there they lay, in the advancing, retreating waves of flick-
ering red light: two enormous pods already burst open in one or
two places, and I reached in with both hands, and tumbled them
out onto the dirt. They were weightless as children's balloons,
harsh and dry on my palms and fingers. At the feel of them on
my skin, I lost my mind completely, and then I was trampling
them, smashing and crushing them under my plunging feet and
legs, not even knowing that I was uttering a sort of hoarse,
meaningless cry—"Unhh! Unhh! Unhh!"—of fright and animal
disgust.

No friendly old men holding up signs reading STOP AND
BE FRIENDLY here; here we have Miles and Jack, mostly
out of their minds, doing the funky chicken over these
weird and insensate invaders from space. There is no discussion (vis-à-vis *The Thing*) of what we could learn from
these things to the benefit of modern science. There is no
white flag here, no parley; Finney's aliens are as strange
and as ugly as those bloated leeches you sometimes find
clinging to your skin after swimming in still ponds. There
is no reasoning here, nor any effort to reason; only Miles's
blind and primitive reaction to the alien outsider.

The book which most closely resembles Finney's is Robert
A. Heinlein's *The Puppet Masters;* like Finney's novel, it is
perhaps nominally SF but is in fact a horror novel. In this
one invaders from Saturn's largest moon, Titan, arrive on
Earth, ready, willing, and able to do business. Heinlein's
creatures are not pods; they are the leeches in actuality.
They are sluglike creatures that ride on the backs of their
hosts' necks the way that you or I might ride a horse. The
two books are similar—strikingly so—in many ways.
Heinlein's narrator begins by wondering aloud if "they"
were truly intelligent. He ends after the menace has been
defeated. The narrator is one of those building and man-

ning rocketships aimed at Titan; now that the tree has been chopped down, they will burn the roots. "Death and destruction!" the narrator exults, thus ending the book.

But what exactly is the threat which the pods in Finney's novel pose? For Finney, the fact that they will mean the end of the human race seems almost secondary (pod people have no interest in what an old acquaintance of mine likes to refer to as "doing the trick"). The real horror, for Jack Finney, seems to be that they threaten all that "nice"—and I think this is where we came in. On his way to his office not too long after the pod invasion is well launched, Miles describes the scenery this way:

> ... the look of Throckmorton Street depressed me. It seemed littered and shabby in the morning sun, a city trash basket stood heaped and unemptied from the day before, the globe of an overhead streetlight was broken, and a few doors down... a shop stood empty. The windows were whitened, and a clumsily painted For Rent sign stood leaning against the glass. It didn't say where to apply, though, and I had a feeling no one cared whether the store was ever rented again. A smashed wine bottle lay in the entranceway of my building, and the brass nameplate set in the gray stone of the building was mottled and unpolished.

From Jack Finney's fiercely individualistic point of view, the worst thing about the Body Snatchers is that they will allow the nice little town of Santa Mira to turn into something resembling a subway station on Forty-second Street in New York. Humans, Finney asserts, have a natural drive to create order out of chaos (which fits well enough with the book's paranoid themes). Humans want to improve the universe. These are old-fashioned ideas, perhaps, but Finney is a traditionalist, as Richard Gid Powers points out in his introduction to the Gregg Press edition of the novel.

From where Finney stands, the scariest thing about the pod people is that chaos doesn't bother them a bit and they have absolutely no sense of aesthetics: this is not an invasion of roses from outer space but rather an infestation of ragweed. The pod people are going to mow their lawns for a while and then give it up. They don't give a shit about the crabgrass. They aren't going to be making any trips down to the Santa Mira True Value Hardware so they can turn that musty old basement annex into a rec room in the best do-it-yourself tradition. A salesman who blows into town complains about the state of the roads. If they aren't patched soon, he says, Santa Mira will be cut off from the world. But do you think the pod people are going to lose any sleep over a little thing like that? Here's what Richard Gid Powers says in his introduction about Finney's outlook:

With the hindsight afforded by Finney's later books, it is easy to see what the critics overlooked [when they] interpreted both the book and the movie... simply as products of the anti-Communst hysteria of the McCarthyite fifties, a know-nothing outburst against "alien ways of life" ... that threatened the American way. Miles Bennell is a precursor of all the other traditionalist heroes of Jack Finney's later books, but in The Body Snatchers, *Miles's town of Santa Mira, Marin County, California still is the unspoiled mythical* gemeinschaft *community that later heroes have had to travel through time to recapture. When Miles begins to suspect that his neighbors are no longer real human beings and are no longer capable of sincere human feelings, he is encountering the beginning of the insidious modernization and dehumanization that faces later Finney heroes as an accomplshed fact.*

Miles Bennell's victory over the pods is fully consistent with the adventurers of subsequent Finney characters: his resistance to depersonalization is so fierce that the pods finally give up on their

*plans for planetary colonization and mosey off to another planet
where the inhabitants' hold on their self-integrity is not so strong.*

Further on, Powers has this to say about the archetypical
Finney hero in general and the purposes of this book in
particular:

*Finney's heroes, particularly Miles Bennell, are all inner-directed
individualists in an increasingly other-directed world. Their
adventures could be used as classroom illustrations of Tocqueville's
theory about the plight of a free individual in a mass democracy.... The Body Snatchers is a raw and direct mass-market version of the despair over cultural dehumanization that fills T. S.
Eliot's Wasteland and William Faulkner's The Sound and the
Fury. Finney adroitly uses the classic science fiction situation of
an invasion from outer space to symbolize the annihilation of the
free personality in contemporary society... he succeeded in creating
the most memorable of all pop cultural images of what Jean
Sheperd was describing on late-night radio as "creeping meatbal-
lism": fields of pods that hatch into identical, spiritless, emotional
vacuous zombies—who look so damned much just like you and
me!*

Finally, when we examine *The Body Snatchers* in light of
the Tarot hand we have dealt ourselves, we find in Finney's
novel almost every damned card. There is the Vampire, for
surely those whom the pods have attacked and drained of
life have become a modern, cultural version of the undead,
as Richard Gid Powers points out; there is the Werewolf,
for certainly these people are not really people at all, and
have undergone a terrible sea change; the pods from space,
a totally alien invasion of creatures who need no space-
ships, can certainly also fit under the heading of the Thing
Without a Name... and you might even say (if you wanted

to stretch a point, and why the hell not?) that citizens of Santa Mira are no more than Ghosts of their former selves these days.

Not bad legs for a book which is "just a story."

Jack Finney and Kevin McCarthy.

THE FICTION OF JACK FINNEY

— — —

Jon L. Breen

Milwaukee-born Walter Braden Finney (1911-1995), professionally known as Jack, was one of the best and most successful writers of popular fiction in the second half of the twentieth century. That may sound like hyperbole—certainly many writers have written more bestsellers and made their names more familiar to the public—but it's an easy statement to defend.

Consider this: each of Finney's four novels of the fifties was serialized in a high-paying slick magazine; each of them was actually filmed successfully; and at least one of the films is considered a classic of its genre. His fifth novel, written with a particular star in mind, was adapted to film with that star in place. A later novel, though never filmed at least partly because of the expense that would be required to do it justice, has become a beloved modern classic.

Does this record of success mean Finney had a rare affinity with the popular taste of his times? Yes. Does it mean he wrote his books with one eye on the possibility of a screen adaptation? Yes, he readily admitted it. Does it mean he was a hack who pandered to his audience, adjusting his viewpoint to coincide with theirs? No. Does it mean he hit on a workable formula and repeated it from book to book? Anything but. Does it mean he wrote screen treatments and published them disguised as novels? Decidedly not. Few writers could have it both ways, attaining outstanding commercial success while being true to a consistent artistic vision, as completely as Jack Finney.

Finney might be likened to Earl Derr Biggers, a popular writer earlier in the century who also had a sensibility uncannily attuned to what the public wanted and the ability to deliver it in a natural, uncontrived way. Unlike Biggers, who is best remembered for his creation of detective Charlie Chan, Finney almost never returned to the same cast of characters. He did, however, have a recurring theme that turned up even in the most unexpected corners of his work: that American life is gradually, sometimes subtly, sometimes dramatically, changing for the worse; that only a few years ago, times were simpler but richer; people were more innocent, more optimistic, more joyful; lives had more purpose and were more fully lived; things were just, well, better all around, not just when we were younger but when the country and the world were younger. Finney's protagonists are afflicted with a sweet but painful nostalgia, a longing for a time or a place or a mood other than their own. (Continuing for a moment the comparison with Biggers, consider the nostalgic view conveyed in *The House Without a Key* of Honolulu, now [in 1925] ruined by tourism and commercialism but a paradise in the relatively recent 1880s.)

While Finney's two most famous works are undoubtedly *The Body Snatchers (1955),* thanks to the two successful film versions, and *Time and Again (1970),* for the richness of his time-travel plot, he produced in his half-century career a wide variety of crime, fantasy, mainstream fiction, and science fiction in which he often returned to his familiar theme of wistful nostalgia but, in subject matter and approach, almost never repeated himself.

Finney's first published story, "The Widow's Walk," appeared in *Ellery Queen's Mystery Magazine* in July 1947. According to the introduction by editor Queen (Frederic Dannay):

> *Mr. Finney is thirty-five years old, married, has no children, and lives in Manhattan. At present he is a copywriter in the advertising agency of Dancer-Fitzgerald-Sample—he has been writing advertising copy for the past twelve years. The EQMM Annual Contest spurred him to write fiction, almost the only writing he has done outside of his work since he finished college in 1934.... [N]ow he is tilting his typewriter at the windmill of radio. His first attempt at radio ratiocination is, in his own words, "quite a bloody script—two killings in less than) fifteen minutes" (which is certainly par for the course).*

I'm not sure how much radio writing Finney actually did—probably not very much, since it didn't take him long to establish himself in the far more lucrative slick magazine market.

In a concluding note, EQ credits "The Widow's Walk," a domestic crime short story of the type later dramatized on Alfred Hitchcock's TV program, with "two of the most important elements in a detective story": a clue and fair play to the reader. The story is the first-person account of a young woman named Annie contemplating the murder of her invalid mother-in-law. Its wickedly clever surprise twist makes it a classic of the type, and editor Queen's claim of fair play is borne out.

Finney appeared only twice more in *EQMM*. In introducing a November 1951 reprint of the 1948 *Collier's* story "It Wouldn't Be Fair," EQ describes the story as a parody of

classical detective fiction. Again, the main character is
named Annie, but quite a different Annie. The mystery-
obsessed girlfriend of New York cop Charley, she "often
solves cases a full forty-eight pages before Perry Mason,"
and her disdain for the intelligence of real-life police puts a
crimp in their romance. While showing its author a
knowledgeable devotee of the kind of pure detective fiction
he seldom ventured to write, the story also demonstrates
the qualities Queen's introduction claims for Finney's fiction: "Jack Finney has developed a slick, sophisticated,
streamlined style; his dialogue is bright; his situations are
genuinely amusing; his characters combine warmth and
gaiety—and who can resist those qualities these cold and
gloomy days?"

Finney's continuing theme of longing for a world outside
one's present reality is manifest in both stories: the first
Annie's for her happy pre-mother-in-law married life, the
second Annie's for the comforting (and *fair*) world of classical detective fiction. For one Annie, a reasonable compro-
mise solution presents itself; for the other, there is only
despair.

Finney's third and last *EQMM* appearance is "The Other
Arrow," a January 1956 reprint of a 1952 story written
with F. M. Barratt and originally published in *Collier's* as
"Diagnosis Completed." Described as a medical mystery in
the Dr. Thorndyke/Dr. Coffee mode, it also includes a
Queenian dying message from the murder victim, a phar-
macist's diabetic wife. The relationship of retiring Dr. Lerner and his young replacement Dr. Knapp is in the great tradition of medical fiction and drama. Dr. Lerner's old-
fashioned view of general medical practice, complete with
house calls, even more remote now than at the time the
story was first published, carries the theme of longing for a
better time.

The fact that *EQMM* never published a second Finney original is accounted for by his remarkable record of success selling to the major American slick magazines. Between 1947 and 1962, he contributed (by my quick count) fifty-three short stories and three serialized novels to those slicks indexed in *Reader's Guide to Periodical Literature*. Initially *Collier's* was his major market; after that publication's mid-fifties demise, he became a regular first in *Good Housekeeping* and finally in *McCall's*, with scattered contributions to *Ladies' Home Journal*, *Cosmopolitan*, and *Saturday Evening Post*. At least one of his later stories, "Hey, Look at Me!", would appear in *Playboy*, equally well-paying but not indexed by the conservative *Reader's Guide*. While his *genre* stories—crime, fantasy, and science fiction—often had a later life, his unreprinted works of general fiction—with tantalizing titles like "Breakfast in Bed" *(Collier's*, May 15, 1948), "My Cigarette Loves Your Cigarette" *(Collier's*, September 30, 1950), and "Husband at Home" *(LHJ*, April, 1951)—illustrate the impermanence of most magazine fiction.

In Finney's most famous short stories, the science fiction and fantasy tales collected in *The Third Level* (Rinehart, 1957) and *I Love Galesburg in the Springtime* (Simon and Schuster, 1963), the nostalgia for a past better and happier than the present is usually conveyed through time-travel situations that foreshadow his definitive treatment of that device in *Time and Again*. In the first volume's title story, the 1950s narrator happens upon a third level of Grand Central Station where the year is 1894—unable to buy a ticket to idyllic Galesburg, Illinois, with his odd-looking new-style money, he returns to the present and ends the story searching for the third level and failing to find it. The final twist is a tribute to Finney's storytelling savvy and a note especially appropriate to the fifties. (How ironic that the period Finney's heroes so often want to escape from is the one that many of today's nostalgics would like to go back to!)

Finney continues his romanticization of Galesburg, where he had attended Knox College, at greater length in the title tale of the second volume of short stories. Beginning with a businessman telling the reporter/narrator about his decision not to build a factory in Galesburg following his encounter with a ghost streetcar, the story concerns the efforts of the past city to resist encroachments of the present.

Brilliant as he is in the short story form, Finney may be even better as a novelist. As Marcia Muller writes in *1001 Midnights* (Arbor, 1986), Finney "has the unusual ability to create edge-of-the-chair tension and sustain it throughout a long narrative." This knack is well-demonstrated in his first novel, *Five Against the House,* serialized in *Good Housekeeping* in 1953, and published in book form by Doubleday the following year.

Nineteen-year-old narrator Al Mercer, like his creator at an earlier time, is a small-college student in Illinois. Beginning on one boring rainy day, he joins three at-loose-ends fraternity brothers to plot a crime. At first, it is to be a Brinks truck robbery, but after an embarrassing encounter with the police while following such a truck, they decide instead to return to Reno, where they had all worked the previous summer, to knock over Harold's Club. They are helped in their planning by Al's waitress girlfriend Tina Greyleg.

Five Against the House is a big caper novel, but it's an amateur caper, generally more interesting (to this reader at least) than a professional one. Most of the conspirators, especially Al and Tina, are presented sympathetically. Al offers Tina this rather strained rationalization for the robbery:

"I think gambling is wrong. People have learned that everywhere, and gambling's been outlawed nearly everywhere in all civilizations. Now, just because a handful of men in the state of Nevada make it technically legal, doesn't make it right. Hell, gambling's wrong and you know it. A few people profit, giving nothing and doing nothing in exchange. And I think everyone concerned is harmed by it....

"So I say they're fair prey.... I feel I'm honest, and wouldn't steal. But to me this isn't stealing; by any standard I respect, that money doesn't belong to Harold's Club, and I'll take it if I can, and it will never bother my conscience for a moment." (Doubleday, page 52)

Finney's technique, repeated in later caper novels, is to hint at the group's method but withhold details until the crime itself is carried out. The author's nostalgic bent is displayed in an imprecation to value the ordinary, as when the Reno conspirators are crossing the country imprisoned in a trailer and value their rare nighttime forays outside, as well as the turns at the wheel that permit them to see ordinary things with fresh eyes.

While a big caper novel about knocking over a gambling casino sounds like pure fiction noir, Finney's slick-paper style somewhat lightens the mood. As in most of his later books, the view of sexuality is very restrained by contemporary standards, reflecting (in common with most of his happy endings) a fifties movie sensibility. But one of the darkest moments in Finney's work comes when a policeman offers the boys a harrowing description of the future he sees for them in prison.

Finney's second novel, *The Body Snatchers*, was serialized in *Collier's* (November 26-December 24, 1954) and published in expanded form as a Dell paperback original in 1955. In many ways, the novel is closely followed in Don

Siegel's 1956 film *Invasion of the Body Snatchers*. In fact, quite a bit of Finney's dialogue was transferred directly into Daniel Mainwaring's script, and of course the central situation is unchanged. But in some very important ways, the two versions differ. Both are classics, but not necessarily for the same reasons.

The Body Snatchers includes the familiar Finney paean to small-town America and old-fashioned doctoring, the latter in the person of Santa Mira general practitioner Miles Bennell, a character even more given to kidding and wisecracks on the page than as played on the screen by Kevin McCarthy. Miles is asked by old girlfriend, now fellow divorcée, Becky Driscoll to look into her cousin Wilma's claims that her beloved uncle Ira is not really her uncle, though no change in his manner, appearance, or memory is apparent. Miles finds similar cases are epidemic in the little town. Gradually the truth is revealed: extraterrestrials have come to earth in the form of giant seed pods and taken over the bodies of the townspeople, turning them into emotionless automatons whose mimicking of human memory, appearance, and mannerisms is not quite good enough to fool sensitive friends and relatives.

While the film is rightly credited with reflecting the anti-communist paranoia of the fifties, the novel's mood is different. It is more a cerebral science-fictional mystery, the greater space afforded by print allowing for speculation and theorizing about the problem at hand that the film has no time for. When a partially formed pod creature is found in the basement of Miles's writer friend Jack Belicec, there is more consideration and discussion of what the phenomenon means and what to do about it. When psychiatrist Mannie Kaufman (Dan in the film) presents his theory of mass hysteria, he offers several historical cases to support his claim.

Some of the most striking scenes in the book are not in the film at all. When Miles and Becky are trapped in his office, with pods waiting to replicate them when they fall asleep, he concocts an ingenious way to misdirect the pods through the use of his two office skeletons. A particularly chilling scene finds Miles and Becky visiting the public library to research newspaper references to the giant seed pods, only to find that the beloved town librarian Miss Wyandotte is among those who have been snatched. One astonishing passage offers a harsh snapshot of American race relations, as Miles compares the changes in the snatched townspeople to an unexpected view of a black shoeshine man's bitter reality.

Introducing the 1976 Gregg Press reprint of *The Body Snatchers*, Richard Gid Powers describes Miles Bennell and other Finney heroes as "inner-directed individuals in an increasingly other-directed world... [whose] adventures could be used as classroom illustrations of Tocqueville's theory about the plight of the free individual in mass democracy." He goes on to sum up the achievement of Finney's first novel as "a raw and direct mass-market version of the despair over cultural dehumanization that fills T. S. Eliot's *Wasteland* and William Faulkner's *The Sound and the Fury*. Finney adroitly uses the classic science fiction situation of an invasion from outer space to symbolize the annihilation of the free personality in contemporary society." (page xi).

Finney's third novel and second paperback original, *The House of Numbers* (Dell, 1957), was the expanded version of a magazine short story *(Cosmopolitan, July 1956)*. The first-person narrator this time is twenty-six-year-old Benjamin Harrison Jarvis, who finds himself in the surprising position of assisting his brother Arnie's escape from San Quentin. Thus, it's the second of the author's three big caper novels, and like the other two is based on in-depth research into its background. As Marcia Muller writes in *1001 Midnights*, "Finney knows San Quentin, although his view of it is colored by his association with then-warden Harley O. Teets, a humanitarian administrator to whom the book is dedicated. (In fact, the dialogue of the fictional warden reads a lot like a public relations release.)"

The third of the big caper books, *Assault on a Queen* (Simon and Schuster, 1959), was serialized in the *Saturday Evening Post* (August 22-September 26, 1959) as "U-19's Last Kill." It begins with a third-person prologue in which Frank Lauffnauer, formerly a German submarine crewman in World War I, rediscovers his old ship sunk off Fire Island. But most of the story is told by a typical Finney narrator, twenty-six-year-old network publicist Hugh Brittain, whose pervasive dissatisfaction with his empty life leads him to quit his job and join some other navy veterans in an elaborate crime: refurbishing the old submarine and using it to rob the Queen Mary. Once again, Finney's amateur criminals try to show they aren't really evil people by offering justification for an *almost* victimless crime. Vic DeRossier, the old navy buddy who is trying to bring Hugh into the caper, likens the caper to knocking over a house party of the very rich:

[E]*very last person there is either out-and-out wealthy, very well off, or making a slug of money. Every one of them, Hugh, or they wouldn't be there. Would you take a few hundred dollars from each of them, if you could? It'd be illegal, all right; a crime, and yet—every single one of them could easily afford it. It'd mean no more to them than losing fifty cents to you.... To you, though, it would make all the difference in the world; you'd be closer to rich, to having the kind of life you want than you ever will be otherwise."* (pages 38-39)

As the conspirators, including of course one beautiful woman, take on the job of getting the submarine back in working order, Finney drives home his customary theme in a passage that may also explain the rarity of sports references in his nostalgic reveries:

There is an enormous loss we all of us suffer, growing up—we stop playing. The things adults call play very seldom are. With hardly an exception they're competitions, even hunting or fishing, even golf, all alone. Rarely ever again do we experience pure play, doing something for its own sake completely, utterly absorbed and lost in it, nothing else mattering. (page 704)

The main character of *Good Neighbor Sam* (Simon and Schuster, 1963) was created with Jack Lemmon in mind. In case anyone missed the envisioned casting, the jacket copy unsubtly compares Finney's comic novel to *Some Like It Hot* and *The Apartment*. Sam Bissell is a twenty-nine-year-old copywriter for the San Francisco advertising firm of Burke & Hare. He is married to Minerva (Min), a twenty-five-year-old brunette who, in the manner of Finney heroines, thinks she is too heavy but really isn't. Their sexy neighbor Janet needs a husband in order to inherit her grandfather's fortune. Since her divorce is pending, her lawyer argues she is still married under strict interpretation of the will, though the other legatees could argue she was not married according to the *spirit* of the will. When Janet's cousins come to visit, Jack (his wife ever understanding) is pressed into service as the neighbor's husband. Finney handles the farcical events to follow with a flawless comic touch and along the way presents some pointed satire on his former profession of advertising, having much fun with campaigns on behalf of Nesfresh eggs and a nostrum called "BELS for the belly." One slogan on behalf of a client's product is wisely rejected at the source:

"SCIENTIFIC TESTS PROVE! THE ONLY CIGARETTE
THAT PRODUCES BENIGN TUMORS!" (page 144).

Good Neighbor Sam is pure comedy and the first Finney
book that can't be easily pigeonholed in the crime, fantasy,
or SF genres. However, a comic turn by an inept private
eye and the con game aspect of the plot *almost* nudge it
into the crime fiction category.

Finney continued in a farcical vein in *The Woodrow Wilson Dime* (Simon and Schuster, 1968), expanded from the
short story "The Coin Collector," originally published in
the *Saturday Evening Post* (January 30, 1960) as "The Other
Wife" and included in Finney's second collection, *I Love
Galesburg in the Springtime*. The hero is another advertising
copywriter, New Yorker Ben Bennell (note the last name),
whose discovery of the titular coin allows him to cross over
into a recognizable but somewhat altered parallel universe.

His next novel, the illustrated *Time and Again* (Simon and
Schuster, 1970), is Finney's finest achievement. Narrator
Simon Morley, an advertising illustrator, is recruited by a
top secret government project created to test Einstein's theory of time. The evocation of Einstein means the events of
the novel, outrageous as they may seem, can arguably be
classified as science fiction rather than pure fantasy. As
project director Dr. Danziger, a Harvard theoretical physi-
cist, explains it:

"[W]e're mistaken in our conception of what the past, present
and future really are. We think the past is gone, the future hasn't
yet happened, and that only the present exists. Because the present is all we can see.... [W]e're like people in a boat without oars
drifting along a winding river. Around us we see only the present.
We can't see the past, back in the bends and curves behind us.
But it's there.... [A] man ought to be able to step out of that boat

onto the shore. And walk back to one of the bends behind us."
(page 52)

The means to achieve this turning backward in time consists of finding a place unaltered since the period you want to visit and surrounding yourself with objects and information from that time. Thus, Si Morley is set up in an apartment in the Dakota, an old New York apartment building on the edge of Central Park, where he steeps himself in New York of the 1880s, reading contemporary newspapers and magazines; using furniture and household appliances, growing whiskers and wearing clothes appropriate to the period; determinedly thinking himself into the targeted place and time. And eventually, he carries his camera and sketch pad into the wonderland of New York in 1882.

In this novel, Finney's rare ability to describe rooms and their contents, and street scenes in all their detail, achieves its ultimate application. Period photographs and drawings are reproduced to help the process, but the magic of the writing does most of the work. A passage describing a walk along Fifth Avenue captures the scene and the time traveler's sense of wonder:

The cross streets slipped by—Forty-ninth, Forty-eighth, Forty-seventy, Forty-sixth—all strange unfamiliar identical streets of uninterrupted row after row of high stooped brownstones precisely like blocks still existing on the West Side. As we'd moved down toward the thick of the city, the street became more and more alive. There they were now, moving along the walks, crossing the street—the people. And I looked out at them, at first with awe, then with delight; at the bearded, cane-swinging men in tall shiny silk hats, fur caps like mine, high-crowned derbies like the man's across the aisle, and—younger men—in very shallow low-crowned derbies. Almost all of them wore ankle-length great coats

*or topcoats, half the men seemed to wear pince-nez glasses, and
when the older men, the silk-hatted men, passed an acquaintance,
each touched his hat brim in salute with the head of his cane. The
women were wearing head scarf or hats ribbon-tied under the
chin; wearing short, tight-waisted cutaway Winter coats, or capes
or brooch-pinned shawls; some carried muff and some wore
gloves; all wore button shoes darting out from and disappearing
under long skirts.*

*There—well, there they were, the people of the stiff old wood-
cuts, only... these moved. The swaying coats and dresses there on
the walks and crossing the streets before and behind us were of
new-dyed cloth—maroon, bottle green, blue, strong brown,
unfaded blacks—and I saw the shimmer of light and shadow in
the appearing and disappearing long folds. And the leather and
rubber they walked in pressed into and marked the slush of the
street crossings; and their breaths puffed out into the winter air,
momentarily visible. And through the trembling, rattling glass
panes of the bus we heard their living voices, and heard a girl
laugh aloud. Looking out at their winter flushed faces, I felt like
shouting .for joy. (page 121; ellipses Finney's)*

Half of Finney's writing life remained after *Time and
Again*, but he would be considerably less prolific. He would
produce four more books at widening intervals in the
quarter century remaining to him. All have their attrac-
tions, but they are inevitably somewhat anticlimactic after
his masterpiece.

Marion's Wall (Simon and Schuster, 1973) returns to the
young, married suburban ambiance of *Good Neighbor Sam*.
Thirty-year-old narrator Nick Cheyney, an employee of
Crown Zellerbach, and wife Jan are peeling wallpaper in
their new apartment in an old San Francisco house when
they unearth a 1926 message from a former tenant: silent
film actress Marion Marsh, once the lover of Nick's father

when he lived in the same building. A public TV viewing of Marion's silent film appearance causes the ghost of the actress, who died in a car crash in the roaring twenties when her film career had only just begun, to materialize. She inhabits the body of Jan to attempt a movie comeback, and later Nick is himself possessed by the shade of Rudolph Valentino. The novel is a valentine (no pun intended) to silent movies and movie collectors—for Nick, a prime mcguffin is the lost reels of Erich Von Stroheim's famous film *Greed*. The novel depicts an earlier era for film buffs, a pre-video period when viewing was often tied to one-shot TV showings and the only chance to own a film was to buy comparatively expensive eight-millimeter prints from a Blackhawk catalog. (When the novel was reprinted along with *The Woodrow Wilson Dime* and *The Night People* in the 1987 omnibus *Three by Finney,* the action was mis-guidedly updated to 1985, making total nonsense of the chronology and the film-collecting references.)

The Night People (Doubleday, 1977) also involves Northern California suburbanites. Lew Joliffe, an apartment-dwelling San Francisco lawyer, is a transplanted midwesterner nostalgic for snow. At night, he takes solitary walks and does odd things (like lying down in the lanes of a freeway or acting out pitching on a Little League mound) without the knowledge of his girlfriend Jo Dunne. With Harry and Shirley Levy—he's another lawyer attracted to daredevil stunts and generally harmless pranks—Lew and Jo form the titular Night People, whose final stunt, involving scaling the superstructure of the Golden Gate Bridge, is a lulu. For some reason, though, these characters, four slow-rising yuppies who need to get a life, are less endearing than the author's usual. It may be that Finney's decision (otherwise unprecedented in the novels) to write in the third person damaged the kind of tenuous reader identification needed to render his central characters likeable.

By this time, Finney was taking more and more time between books. His penultimate work, *Forgotten News: The Crime of the Century and Other Lost Stories* (Doubleday, 1983), is his only nonfiction book, a volume that had its roots in the research for *Time and Again.* Beginning with an appreciation of the woodcut illustrations in *Frank Leslie's Weekly,* Finney goes on to recount at length the 1857 murder case of dentist Harvey Burdell, culminating in the trial of Emma Cunningham for the crime, and slightly more briefly the sinking of the steamship *Central America* in the same year. As in most of his fiction, Finney employs the first person, describing the way he did his research and his reactions to what he found in the 1857 files of the *New York Times* and *Leslie's.* The book is extensively illustrated in a style similar to *Time and Again.*

From Time to Time (Simon and Schuster, 1995) makes Simon Morley a series character, the only one in Finney's canon. Morley, who stayed in New York of the 1880s at the end of *Time and Again,* now visits 1912 in an effort to prevent World War I. The *Titanic* is also involved in the plot. In reviewing the novel in *EQMM* (September 1995), I remarked, "The sequel isn't quite up to the original—the contrivances that set the story in motion are somewhat strained, and the plot seems an excuse for the musings on time and social history—but Finney's unique touch disarms criticism. Like its predecessor, the novel makes an effective use of period photographs and drawings. The glimpse into the life of vaudeville performers, though only slightly related to the story, is especially memorable."

Why has Finney the writer been so much less well-known than the books and stories he wrote? For one thing, he was somewhat reclusive, rarely giving interviews and never (at least to my knowledge) appearing at fan conventions. While not quite a popular fiction equivalent of Thomas Pynchon or J. D. Salinger, he clearly believed the work should speak for itself. Secondly, he had a disdain for being pigeonholed in a genre. His attempt to reach a wider slick-magazine readership with adaptations of science fictional concepts developed over the years in the pulps and digests did not endear him to the SF community, which often disdains such efforts. And accomplished as he was in the crime fiction field, he effectively left it after *Assault on a Queen* to produce works that often drew on several popular genres—romance, fantasy, mystery, science fiction, comedy—at once. Such mixing of categories, now routine in the works of best-selling writers like Stephen King and Dean Koontz, was far less common in the sixties and seventies and certainly militated against brand-name identification.

One supposes all of this mattered little to Finney, who apparently made enough money to write what he wanted to and take as much time as he needed to do it. Any writer offered the chance to make a financial killing *and* write a couple of modern classics along the way would probably take it, even if (maybe, in Finney's case, *especially* if) relative personal anonymity was part of the package.

Don Siegel directs Kevin McCarthy and Dana Wynter in a scene for Invasion of the Body Snatchers (1956)

OF TIME AND PODS: THE FANTASTIC WORLD OF JACK FINNEY

— — —

Fred Blosser

In Jack Finney's universe, the extraordinary and the mundane are not two separate and mutually exclusive conditions of existence.

The first consistently erupts into the second. One merges with the other.

Miles Bennell from *The Body Snatchers* can vouch for that. So can Si Morley, Nick Cheyney, Ben Jarvis, Lew Jollife, and all of Finney's other protagonists.

In Finney's universe, you discover that space aliens have overrun your sleepy hometown, and they look just like— hell, they *are*—your sweetheart, your best friend, the kindly old retiree down the street. You travel back in time to the New York City of the 1880s to solve the mystery of a peculiar carving on a gravestone. You realize that your wife has been possessed by the ghost of a flamboyant silent movie actress. You break into San Quentin Penitentiary....

One of the characters in *The Body Snatchers* says: "We all prefer the weird and thrilling to the dull and commonplace. . . ." Recognizing this basic fact of human nature, Finney was a genius in conveying the emotional jolt that comes when the commonplace suddenly turns into the bizarre.

For some, like Si Morley and Lew Jollife, embracing the extraordinary is a matter of choice. Others, like Miles Bennell and Nick Cheyney, simply have no say in the matter.

Of Finney, Ed Gorman wrote: "To my generation of fantasy and suspense writers, he will always be one of the most important of literary gods." Born Walter Braden Finney in Milwaukee in 1911, this master of the strange and the ordinary sold his first short story to *Ellery Queen's Mystery Magazine* in 1946. His first novel, *5 Against the House,* followed in 1954.

The five of the title are four bored college students—Al, Jerry, Guy, and Brick—and Al's girlfriend, Tina, who together plan and pull a heist at a Reno gambling casino. The scheme is worked out with the ingenuity and attention to realistic detail that were consistent hallmarks of Finney's writing.

Big heist novels were a popular genre in the fifties, but they mostly dealt with hard-boiled professional thieves who approach robbery as a business. Finney pioneered a new subgenre in which everyday amateurs team to pull off a big job as a kick or an intellectual challenge. Others would follow Finney's lead in the late fifties and sixties with movies and books like *The Thomas Crown Affair* (Avon, 1968), *Ocean's 11* (Cardinal, 1960), *Gambit* (Viking Press, 1962), and many more.

In *The Body Snatchers* (1955; revised version, 1978), Finney turns from crime to science fiction. Small-town doctor Miles Bennell discovers that Santa Mira, California (Mill Valley, in the 1978 revision) has been overrun by creatures from outer space that sprout from oversized pods. These invaders replicate the forms and superficial personalities—but not the souls—of the humans with whom they come into contact. And what else can you say about this classic that hasn't already been said better—for example, by Ed Gorman and others elsewhere in this very book? Nothing, probably.

Some critics at the time saw the novel as a McCarthy-era warning about the insidious spread of godless communism. Others interpreted it as a criticism about mindless McCarthyism. Maybe the tale mirrors our fear that the frantic expediencies of modern life are already turning us all into real-life pod people, possessing no more warmth or substance than the images we see on a TV set. "Sometimes," Miles reflects early in the story, "I think we're refining all humanity out of our lives."

Finney himself claimed that the story was meant as entertainment, nothing more. But a later generation of writers would find inspiration for a uniquely twentieth-century school of horror fiction rooted in the quiet terrors of small-town life. It was a lesson taught by Finney, Matheson, Bradbury, and Bloch, and taken to heart by King, Koontz, and Gorman. No longer could you evade monsters by staying clear of Dracula's Transylvania or Lovecraft's decaying New England backwaters. The monsters were coming to *you*, and they were as close as the corner gas station, the local high school, your own backyard.

The House of Numbers (1957) was an inventive return to crime fiction with the patented Finney touch of approaching a familiar genre (in this case, the prison-break story) in a new and different way. When San Quentin inmate Arnie Jarvis faces a possible death sentence in an attack on a guard, he convinces his brother Ben to mount a rescue. To do so, Ben himself must sneak into the prison, take Arnie's place for a day—long enough for the latter to rig an escape route for himself—and then go back over the wall before somebody discovers the deception.

As usual, Finney's setting is impeccably researched, his characters incisively drawn, his stratagems cleverly developed. Who but Finney would have pegged a prison escape on a confusion of identities? When Ben successfully passes himself off as Arnie to a prison guard who has already met him in the outside world as Ben, one is reminded of the chilling impostures of *The Body Snatchers:* "Of course to this man I could only be Arnold Jarvis, the man he knew was an inmate here; naturally Arnold Jarvis would resemble his brother."

Finney was also busy in the 1950s as a writer of short stories for the *Saturday Evening Post, Collier's,* and other popular slicks. These tales were eventually collected in two volumes—*The Third Level* (1957) and *I Love Galesburg in the Springtime* (1963). To single out only a few of these gems, "Contents of a Dead Man's Pockets" is a tense little chiller worthy of de Maupassant and John Collier. "The Third Level," "Of Missing Persons," and "I'm Scared" are fantasy classics, the veritable forerunners of Rod Serling's *Twilight Zone.*

In fact, one wonders. Debuting as it did in the prosaic era of Ike and Norman Vincent Peale, would Serling's TV series have found a receptive audience if Finney hadn't already cultivated millions of readers with his compact parables about time travel, strange disappearances, and doorways to idyllic alien worlds? I think the question is open for discussion.

Ironically, Serling himself would later write the script for the 1966 movie version of Finney's last novel of the fifties. In *Assault on a Queen* (1959), another team of amateurs assembles. Their immediate goal: to raise a German U-boat lost off Long Island in the closing days of World War II. Next step: to use the sub as their vehicle for a raid on the Queen Mary as the luxury liner returns to port with a full complement of wealthy passengers.

Once again, Finney reveals his talent for exploring an arcane subject in fascinating detail while unreeling a tense, fast-paced crime plot. How does a World War I sub operate, and how do you restore it to working order after it's lain untended on the ocean floor after forty years? Finney tells you, and the particulars are worth the price of admission all by themselves.

On top of that, Finney delivers a story line that continually takes the reader by surprise. As Hugh Brittain and his cohorts board the Queen Mary, as rivalry mounts between Hugh and his co-conspirator Ed Marino over the attention of their gorgeous partner Rosa, events never go in quite the direction you expect them to go. Finney never settles for the easy cliché, the familiar plot device.

Finney wrote two novels in the sixties, both dealing with marital crises. But don't expect the suburban angst of John Updike or John Cheever. In *Good Neighbor Sam* (1963), amiable adman Sam agrees to pose as his wife's best friend's husband to help the friend secure an inheritance. The deception spirals hilariously out of control when one of Sam's clients decides to showcase the fraudulent pair as America's perfect couple in a national ad campaign.

The Woodrow Wilson Dime (1968; revised version, 1987) expands upon an earlier short story, "The Coin Collector" (or "The Other Wife," its original title). Benjamin Bennell (Miles's less ambitious younger brother?) is an unfulfilled New York ad writer who has grown bored with his dead-end job and his wife Hetty. One day, a way out of his bind presents itself. A dime stamped with the profile of Woodrow Wilson pays Ben's admission into an alternate universe.

In this world next door, Ben is wealthy, the owner of his own agency, and married to the voluptuous Tessie. It should be paradise, but Finney sardonically points out a basic fact of life for the wistful Ben Bennells of the world, whatever that particular world may be: What you don't have is always what you most desire.

What Ben now wants is his original wife, Hetty. But the alternate-universe Hetty is already engaged to slick patent attorney Custer Huppfelt. The quest to win her back leads Ben to yet another parallel world—one in which he's flat broke and divorced from Hetty, and Custer again stands in the way of romantic bliss—and to a wacky scam that recalls the comedy capers of Donald E. Westlake.

Another unfulfilled adman is the hero of *Time and Again* (1970). "There wasn't anything really wrong with my life," Simon (Si) Morley ponders. "Except that, like most everyone else's I knew about, it had a big gaping hole in it, an enormous emptiness, and I didn't know how to fill it."

Government operative Rube Prine suggests an answer. Scientists have discovered a simple technique for time travel, and Prine offers Si the chance to step back to the New York City of 1882 as a test subject.

The Feds look at time travel strictly as a military device, a way to change the past advantageously for present-day national security. For Si, the Project offers a way to answer a question that has puzzled his lady friend Kate for years: Why did the mailing of a certain letter on January 23, 1882, result years later in the suicide of a New York financier named Andrew Carmody, whose son became Kate's adopted father?

Arguably rivaling *The Body Snatchers* as Finney's most popular work, *Time and Again* is many things, all of them quite wonderful. It's perhaps the most impressive historical novel ever written about everyday urban life in nineteenth-century America. It's an absorbing mystery that turns on Si's pursuit of Andrew Carmody. It's a clever examination of the mechanics and paradoxes of time travel that made mainstream SF safe for moviemakers like Nicholas Meyer with *Time After Time* (1978) and Spielberg and Zemeckis with *Back to the Future* (1985). It's also an appealing love story about Si's romance with Julia, a woman of 1882, and about Finney's own infatuation with a quieter, simpler age of wintry sleigh rides on Fifth Avenue, before the "first of the terrible corrupting wars" of the twentieth century.

There's also a thoughtful subtext that gives the novel an added emotional charge. As Si compares the 1880s with the 1970s and measures the social and technological changes in between, he realizes that society often does terrible things in the name of progress. Too often, the public accepts the self-serving dictates of politicians and corporations without reckoning the consequences. By the time we comprehend our mistakes, it's too late.

As Si meditates, "I was, and I knew it, an ordinary person who long after he was grown retained the childhood assumption that the people who largely control our lives are better informed than, and have judgment superior to, the rest of us.... Not until Vietnam did I finally realize that some of the most important decisions of all time can be made by men knowing really no more than, and who are not more intelligent than, most of the rest of us."

It's a dilemma that resonated with Finney's audience in 1970, the year when National Guardsmen fired on students at Kent State, when disgust over America's befouled lakes, rivers, and air led to historic environmental reforms. It still resonates today, maybe more so than ever—hence the satisfaction the reader feels when Si returns to 1882 to marry Julia and to change the past in one small, critical way that prevents the Project from ever coming into existence....

Marion's Wall (Simon & Schuster, 1973) was Finney's loving tribute to another golden age, the heyday of 1920s

Hollywood and silent movies. When Nick and Jan
Cheyney move into an old Victorian in San Francisco, they
discover a message scrawled on a wall in lipstick under an
old layer of wallpaper—"Marion Marsh lived here. Read it
and weep." Marion was an aspiring actress who died in an
automobile accident in 1927 just after landing her breakthrough movie role. Her ghost still inhabits the house, and
it begins to inhabit Jan's body, too.

This development makes life uncertain for Nick. Whenever he begins to make love to Jan, he can't be sure
whether it's actually her or the flamboyant Marion. One
expects Finney to play this Thorne Smith situation for
risqué humor, and he does. The novel provides some
delightful laughs, along with Finney's charming medita-
tions about the glamorous Hollywood of Valentino, Swan-
son, and Theda Bara. But there's also an echo of Miles Bennell's dilemma in *The Body Snatchers:*

*"This was Jan's face, her dark hair, her arms, hands and body,
but... there was a recklessness in the eyes, a fullness to the smiling
lips, a tension and excitement in every line of that familiar body,
that I'd never seen before.... This was another woman...."*

In *The Night People* (1977), four affluent but bored suburbanites in Mill Valley embark on a progressively more out-
landish and dangerous series of nighttime pranks. They are
counterparts of the restless college students of *5 Against the
House* two decades later, rebelling against the complacency
of a well-paid, comfortable, and rootless existence. As the
main character, Lew Jollife, reflects: "He liked his job—
liked it all right, that is, but could give it up. Liked where
they lived, but could leave. Could give up anything, it
seemed."

The book's big set piece is one of Finney's most gripping:

a nighttime climb by Lew and his friend Harry to the top of the Golden Gate Bridge. But *The Night People* may be most remarkable as a parable of anomie and angst in the comfortable white-collar middle class during the Ford and Carter era, comparable to the free-flowing, absurdist seventies movies of Paul Mazursky and Robert Altman.

Forgotten News (1983) was a nonfiction entertainment about sensational but now-forgotten events of the 1800s, based on Finney's extensive research in period newspapers for *Time and Again*. Along with *About Time (1986)*, a volume of time-travel tales from Finney's earlier short story collections, the book revived popular interest in *Time and Again*. Fans began wondering: Did Simon Morley really give up time travel? Was the Project truly defunct? Finney finally answered those questions twelve years later in his final book.

As *From Time to Time (1995)* opens, we learn that Si Morley wasn't completely successful in altering the past. Scientists piece together evidence that twentieth-century history has unrolled in at least two different but sometimes contiguous tracks. Meanwhile, Rube Prine and others stubbornly pursue subliminal memories of an alternate 1970 in which they launched a time travel experiment called the Project....

Ingeniously, Rube and his colleagues reverse Si's tampering with time and convince Morley to make another foray into the past. The destination is 1912; the mission, to safeguard a shadowy government agent known to history only as "Z." There is a chance to avert World War I if Si can locate Z and keep him from sailing on an ill-fated voyage to Europe—or failing that, if Si can prevent the sinking of the liner on which Z booked his return passage: the *Titanic*.

If the sequel isn't as satisfying as the original, it may be simply that the reader misses the greater profusion of

detail that crowded *Time After Time*. Still, there is much
charm in Finney's description of the old, majestic ocean
liners, and when Si explores the culture of vaudeville and
goes to see a performance by Al Jolson in the flesh, the
reader has the sense of being in a world a little closer to
our own time, a little more familiar than the horse-drawn-
cart setting of the earlier book.

The denouement, as Si desperately tries to alter the
course of the *Titanic*, again points out the perplexing dilem-
mas of time travel. If you could do something to prevent a
monstrous event from happening, would you do it, even if
the other consequences are unguessable? And how do you
know that the action you take won't in fact lead to the
occurrence that you want to avert?

As the book concludes, Si returns for good to the 1880s,
determined never to venture into time again but hopeful of
making small changes to protect his immediate family from
the bad things the future holds in store.

It's a poignant ending, as if Finney, in a personal way,
were saying his own farewell to a full career of exploring
the mundane and the marvellous. Shortly after *From Time
to Time* was published, Jack Finney died, on November 16,
1995.

AN INTERVIEW WITH DANA WYNTER

— — —

Tom Weaver

"I hate the idea of a double," Dana Wynter once told a *TV Guide* interviewer, adding that she always refused to allow herself to be doubled in her movies. She was referring, of course, to the standard use of stunt doubles and stand-ins during picture-making; but for fans of *Invasion of the Body Snatchers* the comment has a coincidental "double" meaning: it vividly recalls her costarring role as Becky Driscoll, the chic divorcée romantically pursued by Kevin McCarthy—then stalked and ultimately duplicated by the extraterrestrial pod people—in the 1956 science fiction classic.

The daughter of a noted surgeon, she was born Dagmar Wynter in Berlin, Germany, and grew up in England. When she was sixteen, her father went to Morocco to perform an operation; he then visited friends in southern Zimbabwe (then Rhodesia), fell in love with it, and brought his daughter and her stepmother to live with him there. Wynter later enrolled as a premed student at Rhodes University (one of two girls in a class of 150 boys) and also dabbled in theatrics there, playing the blind girl in a school production of *Through a Glass Darkly*, in which she says she was "terrible." After a year plus of studies, Wynter

Kevin McCarthy and Dana Wynter

returned to England and shifted gears, dropping her medical studies and turning to an acting career. She was appearing in a play in Hammersmith (the "Q" theatre) when a director of the American agency Famous Artists said he wanted to represent her. She left for New York on November 5, 1953—"Guy Fawkes Day," a holiday commemorating a 1605 attempt to blow up the Parliament building. "The night sky was filled with fireworks," Wynter later told an interviewer, "and I couldn't help thinking it was a fitting send-off for my departure to the New World."

Wynter had more success in New York than in London, with major rôles on TV *(Robert Montgomery Presents, Suspense, Studio One,* among others) and the stage before being summoned to Hollywood and a contract with 20th Century Fox Studio a short time later. The willowy, dark-eyed actress appeared in over a dozen films, was loaned by the studio to *Playhouse 90* in the Golden Age of Television, and later costarred in her own short-lived series with Robert Lansing, *The Man Who Never Was.* Married and divorced from hotshot Hollywood lawyer Greg Bautzer, and with one son, Mark Ragan, Dana Wynter, once called Hollywood's "oasis of elegance," retired from acting and took up journalism with her own by-line for England's oldest newspaper, *The Guardian,* as well as for the *Irish Times, Country Living* and other magazines. Her primary residence is in County Wicklow, Ireland.

Tom Weaver: When you first arrived in New York from England in 1953, things must have been touch-and-go for a while.

Dana Wynter: Yes, I was living on doughnuts, peanuts, whatever happened to be cheap that week… the English only allowed five hundred pounds to be taken out of the country at that time—after that you had to make your own way. But I was very lucky in my friendship with [composer] Richard Rodgers in England, and when I got my first TV show, *Robert Montgomery Presents*, he had rallied helpful people to watch it. I had the lead in the show—by default—Eva Gabor became ill, and they pushed *me* in to replace her. It was one of those miraculous things which happen in America, those wonderful, crazy, no-reason gifts of opportunity. (By the way, on that first show, I thought to myself, "How *kind* Americans are, to employ deaf veterans in television studios." Well, I didn't know that all the floor managers and cameramen had things in their ears for communication with the control booth! I was *that* naive!) But Richard Rodgers got people like [TV producer] Martin Manulis to watch, and after that I was set. *So* lucky. My life has really been blessed, it's all been magical.

Weaver: You also acted in a play in New York, a comedy called *Black-Eyed Susan,* with Vincent Price.

Wynter: Vincent was an enchanting man, highly civilized and passionate about art which he used to teach. Kay Medford was a brilliant comedienne who was generous and patient beyond belief, with me. I'd never done comedy before and kept falling into everybody else's laughs and wasn't getting my own. Awful. But Kay took me in hand with a crash-course in comedy-timing. Well, we got to Boston where Elliot Norton was *the* out-of-town critic at the time—if you got a decent notice from him you were okay for New York, but if not, good-night. Well, I was lucky, got a thumbs-up from him and wasn't fired. We opened on Broadway just before Christmas [1954]—to about five people, all relatives of the cast [laughs]! Quite an experience, I'll tell you. Baptism by fire!*

The very *best* memories of my whole professional life are of the *Playhouse 90* days—I was in three†, two with [director] Johnny Frankenheimer, one with Robert Stevens, and I'll tell you, that was a golden time in American live television. The excitement will never be duplicated—it was a cradle of creativity. I mean, just think of the now famous directors and writers who were discovered and nourished by Martin Manulis and John Houseman in those years.

Weaver: I found a quote from a 1958 interview where you talked about how much you liked live TV—compared with movies.

Wynter: Yes. Quite right. I like the preparation, I *love* the rehearsal period—it was absolutely intense. Total immersion. All were wonder-

---

*[Black-Eyed Susan] is a farce," wrote a *New York Daily News* critic. "It also is a fiasco. Moreover, it is shoddy, sleazy, leering, vulgar, blatant, ill-mannered, coarse, witless, feckless, insulting, discouraging and unfunny." According to the headline of the *New York Times* review, "All Goes Well in *Black-Eyed Susan* until First Actor Steps on Stage.

†*Winter Dreams* (May 23, 1957), *The Violent Heart* (February 6, 1958), and *The Wings of the Dove* (January 8, 1959).

fully professional, and if there was a problem with the writing... anybody's lines... or *anything, everybody* tried to find a way to fix it and make it better. The work was thrilling and totally unique. When we did *Wings of the Dove*, Isabel Jeans was in the cast, a lovely, lovely English actress (who played Audrey's grandmother in *Gigi* [1958]). She looked at me oddly on the first day of rehearsal and she said rather haughtily, "And what role do *you* play, dear?" I had to gently explain that I was playing the lead girl [laughs]!

Well, after a few days we became great friends, and one day she turned to me and said, "I've never *done* live television before, dear. How many people do you suppose *watch* this program *Playhouse 90!*" I said, "I don't exactly know. On a *bad* night, I guess twenty million. On a *good* night, forty million." "Forty million people....? *Forty million people??!!*" Well, after that she was pacing the corridors, gripping script with ever-long-gloved hands, muttering, "Forty million people... oh my God!" Well, we were finally on the air, in the middle of this scene in a conservatory in our lovely period costumes and hats, when half-way through a scene to my horror I saw "forty million people" in her eyes and I thought, "That's it! She's going to 'up,'" and we had a long way yet to go. But the old lady pulled herself together... took a very deep breath... and went on. And she was wonderful. I'll never forget the moment of panic striking her, but her discipline saved the day. *That* was the excitement! When the *Playhouse 90* theme came up at the top of the show, and they were counting down, "ten, nine, eight, seven, six…"—the adrenaline rush was huge… we faced jeopardy—I mean, if anything/anyone went wrong, the disaster involved camera-moves, sponsors and reputation, never mind the disgrace in front of millions.

When we did Daphne du Maurier's *The Violent Heart,* Ben Gazzara and I were playing a scene, all of a sudden out of the corner of my eye I saw something fall with a big thud. It turned out to be the cameraman! We had four cameramen on this live show, an electrician holding a small spot light had leaned against the operator or something, and his light shorted through his camera. The guy got a very sharp electric shock and fell off. Luckily, a cameraman from another set had just wandered onto our set because whenever Johnny Frankenheimer was directing, everybody would come to watch. Crews worshipped him. This other man climbed onto the camera, grabbed the miked headphones saying [to the control booth], "Johnny, I don't know this show, but I'll *try* if you want to talk me through it." Imagine! It was tremendously difficult with all the cables [from four cameras], but Johnny called all the shots, lens-sizes and moves, and we got through the piece without anyone knowing that one of four cameras had been lost. The original guy climbed back on his camera for the last of the six acts. Now, *that* kind of thing never happens in film—it's so *dull* by comparison.

Weaver: You started your Hollywood movie career under contract to Twentieth Century Fox.

Wynter: I was offered a contract by Metro too but luckily Charlie Feldman chose Fox for me. Seven years of happiness there—it was like one big family.

Weaver: Before you appeared in a single Fox movie, you costarred in *Invasion of the Body Snatchers*. Why did producer Walter Wanger think of you?

Wynter: Some time prior to that, I was in the William Morris Agency in New York—I don't know why as they weren't my agents. Probably with a friend. Anyway, Walter Wanger came in, saw me and asked who I was. I didn't meet him at the time.

Weaver: But he thought of you when he went to do *Body Snatchers*.

Wynter: Well, apparently Vera Miles had been penciled in by Allied Artists for the role but Walter Wanger said, "No, I want that new girl. The English one." That's when they found out that I was under contract to Fox, who allowed the start of the contract to be delayed so I could do the picture. *Invasion of the Body Snatchers* was my first film.

Weaver: No, you *were* in some English movies—

Wynter: No, no ... I really wasn't *in* them, you know. I was trying to make a living doing whatever I could while I was studying.

Weaver: So *Body Snatchers* was the first movie you had a sizable role in.

Wynter: Yes.

Weaver: Any "first-picture jitters" on *Body Snatchers,* or had you had enough experience on TV to walk right in and go to work?

Wynter: Not jitters, no, because everybody was awfully nice. Well, *most* people were. From live TV to *this* was a *dawdle,* you know what I mean? You had time to gather yourself together. Acting in film is largely a matter of concentration as Jimmy Stewart once said when we were dinner-partners...and keeping the energy-level correct all the way through. Also, I was quite young and inexperienced, and... well, "fools rush in," you know [laughs]! Ellsworth Fredericks the cameraman was very kind to me, too, and they are key; terribly concerned, always "there," ever friendly and helpful. The crew gathered round and were supportive—I've a feeling it had to do with my English accent.

Weaver: "*Most* people" were nice, you just said. Who *wasn't* nice?

Wynter: I must say I learned a lot from her, but Carolyn Jones was... strangely unfriendly and unhelpful. But I learned a lot from *that*, too, because I became more aware that if there's someone in your cast who's new to the medium and hasn't been around much, you try and help them feel welcome and supported. That was the only... "strange" event.

Weaver: You had to have a plaster cast made of your body for the pod scenes. What was that experience like?

Wynter: Very odd, but worse for Carolyn, because she was claustrophobic. It wasn't that bad for me, apart from the sense of humor of the guys who were making the things. Being encased was like being in a sarcophagus which was steadily heating up. Breathing through straws. Totally covered apart from that and a small aperture for the mouth. Then we heard with a tap on each box, "Listen, we won't be long, we're just off for lunch [laughs]!"

Weaver: One article said it got to be 120 degrees inside that thing.

Wynter: Yes, that plaster heated up, all right!

Weaver: I never quite understood why you and the others had to go through all that, why these dummies had to be made. Why couldn't the actors themselves just lie inside the pods in the scenes where they opened up?

Wynter: Probably because the special effects people weren't as advanced technically as now, and hadn't decided exactly the best way to make it work. Just as well, because weren't a lot of soap-suds involved? Imagine! I only saw that picture once, and that was a very long, long time ago, and I really don't remember the scene with the opening pods I was so bowled over by the brilliance of Kevin McCarthy's performance.

Weaver: Did you read the short story that the movie was based on?

Wynter: Yes. This sounds stupid, but I can't remember any unusual reaction to it. I'll tell you something: once something is *done,* completed, I put it behind me. Maybe it's the Satchel Paige syndrome—"Never look behind you, they may be gaining on you." I guess one remembers the very important things in life, not the minutiae. My career wasn't my passion, and that's why I left. Unlike your superb Ann Bancroft. And Kevin, for instance, who is 100% true actor, it's in the marrow of his bones. For *me,* I tend to skitter about and usually do things out of some foolish intellectual curiosity—to see if I can succeed. Then it's on to something else. When I left "show-biz" I wrote for various magazines and had my own byline for over a year in *The Manchester Guardian.* It's one of Britain's oldest newspapers, and to have a series of my own in it every fortnight— home to my journalist-hero Alistair Cooke, for heaven's sake—was a thrill. Then I had to leave for Zimbabwe for three years to care for my widowed, ill father, and couldn't manage dead-lines. Anyway, once I *did* something, learning to fly—once you fly solo, that's the huge adrenaline kick; after that it's time to move on to something else. I know that's a very flibberty-gibbety way of going about life, but great fun!

Weaver: Walter Wanger—how did you like knowing him?

Wynter: Walter was an extraordinary man, unique in that town because he was so *civilized*, highly educated, well-read, had impeccable good taste and manners. An "original" in Hollywood, but oddly people recognized and respected his qualities. I don't know how he survived in that community.

Weaver: Was he on the set a lot?

Wynter: Yes, quite a bit.

Weaver: He called you "a brunette Grace Kelly with the zest of Ava Gardner. My best discovery since Hedy Lamarr."

Wynter: Typical generosity!

Weaver: In interviews, Don Siegel sometimes told a far-out-sounding story that he once broke into your house and put a pod under your bed.

Wynter: That *is* a bit far-out. Actually, he left it on my doorstep. I lived in an enclave of little cottages near the Mormon Temple on Santa Monica Blvd. and Don was courting my neighbor, Doe Avedon. One night he just left the thing outside my door!

Weaver: And you found it—

Wynter: Well I nearly broke my neck because at five-thirty a.m., on the way to one's car, pod-traps are not uppermost on the mind [laughs]!

Weaver: What was Siegel like as a director?

Wynter: Very interesting. He had so much *fizz* and all, that New York energy. Enthusiasm and drive with a wry sense of humor. It was all good. And he choose Sam Peckinpah to be the dialogue coach.

Weaver: Peckinpah used to give interviews in which he claimed to have rewritten the script of *Body Snatchers.* Finally the real writer got fed up and threatened to sue, and Peckinpah never told that lie again.

Wynter: That's very interesting. He was a quiet, nice man but I have no particular memory of him.

Weaver: According to one of the trade papers, *Body Snatchers* was mostly shot on actual locales, and only four out of the twenty-four days was shot in the studio.

Wynter: That could be right. Bronson Canyon was where Miles goes off and leaves Becky in the tunnel, as well as where the final chase took place. Can you believe, people write *theses* about *Body Snatchers?* It's the damndest thing! One man measured—*measured*—the distance from one corner of the town where we shot, to the other. He actually said to me, "Now, Dana, when you say, "I'm here, Miles," when Kevin McCarthy comes back to the cave. It's a tritonal reading—you go from B-flat to E to G. Now *that* was brilliant. How did you decide upon that tritonal thing?" And I thought to myself, "These people are out of their minds [laughs]!"

Weaver: Have I given you the impression that I'm out of *my* mind yet?

Wynter: [chuckles] *You* sound absolutely wonderful!

Weaver: Did you have a stunt double at any point in those strenuous scenes?

Wynter: No, and poor Kevin—p-o-o-r Kevin—had to carry me! I was quite chunky at the time, but all his good manners were tested—he was *terrific* running in and out of that muddy canyon carrying heavy old me without a huff or a puff or even a grimace!

Weaver: It really looks like a very grueling chase. Was there enough time between shots for everybody to catch their breath, or was it a real hard day?

Wynter: The picture was shot in—what?—three weeks, and there were a lot of setups, so there *wasn't* much time in between. They really got a move on, which was good.

Weaver: After you and Kevin McCarthy hide your-selves beneath the floorboards of the cave, the townspeople swarm in searching for you. At the very end of the shot, one guy steps between the boards and starts to fall forward. Did he fall on top of the two of you?

Wynter: I just remember an awful lot of bits of earth and stones falling on us, but they wouldn't have risked actually leaving us in such a vulnerable position for the whole crowd to trample over the boards. I was sorry for the cameraman who took our place!

Weaver: Was the scene on the giant staircase a hassle?

Wynter: Not really but it could have been if Wanger, Siegel, Ellsworth and the crew were not such professionals. The actors were mostly theater people, so there was no waffling about and not knowing the lines. There wasn't a lot of discussion about motivation, performances were thought through [by the actors themselves] and delivered.

Weaver: Did you have an "approach," or what's the *key* to playing in a far-out movie like *Body Snatchers?* Or didn't your mind work that way?

Wynter: Well you see, *on the surface* nothing was mentioned about it being far-out. It was supposed to be an original, thrilling picture. That was what Allied Artists thought was being made. Having read Philip Wylie's wonderful book, *Generation of Vipers* [1942], I took it for granted that we—Walter, Kevin,

Don Siegel, were all educated people who *can* think about things and knew it was an anti-any-"ism" film. But it wasn't spoken about on the set. They were delicate times, and if Allied Artists had had the slightest idea that there was anything deeper to this movie, it would have quickly been stopped!

Weaver: I don't know if Don Siegel ever owned up to it being an anticommunist movie. I think he always sort of ducked the subject.

Wynter: Well, the story was what it was, and it worked on both levels. So there was no point in saying, "Well, now, look here, what we're really doing is *this*...." Kevin has stories about the humor in the film that was firmly knocked out by Allied—"We don't want any *laughs* in here!" Oh, they were *something,* those people. I tell you, it took some getting used to, being part of that town [Hollywood] when you come from another culture. Values are very odd. I remember having been invited to a house famous for the producer's collection of wonderful paintings. It was the usual thing: dinner and then the guests went to the projection room to watch the latest movie from the studio, pre-release. Out of the corner of my eye I saw a very precious Matisse—plummeting from the library wall, so I yelled, "Watch out!" because a Renoir was appearing to crash down too. Everybody turned to look at me. "What on earth's the matter with *her?*" It didn't occur to me that anyone in their right mind would *nail* masterpieces to flaps to cover the projection-ports. The projectionist would press a button, down they'd go to reveal the port-holes the film was shown through. Barbarians!

Weaver: You just mentioned that the humor was cut out of the movie by Allied Artists. Walter Wanger didn't have enough pull to keep that from happening?

Wynter: I don't know *what* his position was in the studio-system at that time. Perhaps he was just weary. He'd either lost his grip *or*, as Billy Wilder says, "You don't lose your talent in this business, you just become unfashionable." That's pretty good, isn't it? Perhaps the shooting of Jennings Lang* kind of made him into a bit of a laughingstock in that town. Maybe he was just too good for them—too educated and sophisticated, made them feel uncomfortable. That's understandable.

Weaver: Your impressions of Kevin McCarthy?

Wynter: Kevin's unique—as a person and an actor. Totally dedicated to everything he undertakes... generous, unselfish, supportive and full of enthusiasm and encouragement. He's decent through and through, all his instincts are right, and he hides his erudition with great modesty. He has genuine charm with-

---

*In 1951, Wanger, the husband of actress Joan Bennett, convinced himself that Bennett and her agent, Jennings Lang, were having an affair, and he shot and wounded Lang in an office building parking lot. Wanger served a short prison sentence.

out that actor *thing*. I've had very few actor-friends because I can't bear "actor-talk" [laughs]!

Weaver: And you felt that way about him in 1955, as you were making the movie?

Wynter: At that time I'd done a few plays and things but hadn't been that much exposed to the genus of "*ac*-tor." They inevitably try to enlist one against *other* actors in a company; they gang up on each other and/or the director. Theatre gossip is tiresome. Kevin has such *masculinity*—no pettiness either. Well, look at where he comes from—he and his sister [Mary McCarthy] are serious people. Very special.

Weaver: In your early publicity, the first movie you made for Fox, *The View from Pompey's Head* [1955, later re-titled *Secret Interlude*], got all the attention. If *Body Snatchers* was mentioned at all, it was referred to as a "quickie," as something that had to be gotten out of the way before you could start your *real* movie career.

Wynter: It was wonderfully real to me! But that impression came about through the Fox publicity machine, and of course they weren't interested in doing anything for *Body Snatchers*. Also, remember, it was considered a B picture from the start because that's what Allied Artists was known for. The publicity "push" at Fox had to be for *their* new girl. By the way, one movie I made there, *D-Day, the Sixth of June,* was just on here in Ireland—shown on the 6th every year. That was my favorite.

Weaver: Your favorite movie to make, or the best movie you're in?

Wynter: It was the one I really enjoyed the most because it was with Robert Taylor and Richard Todd. We'd been great pals in England before the film, and coming together to make it at Fox was just wonderful. Honestly, this *Body Snatchers* thing—I was new, young, and boring. My acting was *boring.* There was no edge. With luck, you develop a bit of that as you get older, along with a bit of humor. In a first picture, it's all so important that you're terrified of doing the wrong thing that everything's played straight. So it's nothing I'm *proud* of. Now it's become a bit of an albatross. I can see the one line on my headstone— *Body Snatchers.* I wish I could check out of the whole happening.

Weaver: Did you feel, by making a B picture, a science fiction picture, that you were starting off in Hollywood on the wrong foot?

Wynter: Oh, no, it was very much the right foot for me. I was happy because I liked Walter very much—and he had faith in me. Anyway, a first picture's always a thrill. But that title! I begged Walter, "You can't! My *parents!* How can I announce to my parents that I'm doing a picture called *Invasion of the Body Snatchers,* for God's sake! They'll think I'm demented [laughs]!" How do you explain *that* away? Even now, people who don't know it, snicker. Don Siegel fought hard to have it called *Sleep No More.*

Weaver: In 1955, before *Body Snatchers* had been released, you were already telling interviewers that the title was dreadful. You also said about it, "I suppose it will appeal to the science fiction kids."

Wynter: Oh Lord! ...it's terrible you can't *bury* your past, isn't it? It's always there to haunt you!

Weaver: I just thought it was interesting that you were so frank about your own first movie.

Wynter: Well, until you learn "studio speak" and professional hypocrisy, you say things like that. The senior publicity woman at Fox used to appear on the set every day—a nice person but terribly... *insistent.* Pencil poised over paper with, "Now, what did you do last night?" And it used to drive everybody crazy. I remember Robert Taylor finally really *telling* her—he made it up to such a racy degree that she fled, scarlet-faced, and never asked him *that* question again. Being responsible for something fabricated by a studio employee took some getting used to, but contract-players were considered "possessions" and that was that. Outrageous!

Weaver: Once you married Greg Bautzer, obviously you didn't worry about where your next meal was coming from, and yet you stuck with your acting career.

Wynter: I was under contract and Fox wouldn't release me. I begged to be let out, because they wouldn't allow their people to do *anything* [beyond the movie work], especially in television. When Martin Manulis, John Houseman and John Frankenheimer sent me the script for the Scott Fitzgerald *Winter Dreams* [episode of *Playhouse 90*], it was such a wonderful story—part of Americana—that I begged Buddy Adler, the head of Fox at the time, to let me do it. The answer was, "None of our people may do TV." I countered with, "But how do we *learn*, stretch ourselves, if we just go from film to film?" I made such a fuss that he had the grace to read it, the front office held discussions and finally relented. So at least I broke *that* nonsense open—and ended up doing three *Playhouse 90s* while at Fox because after a while they were recognized as being prestigious.

Weaver: But you couldn't get Fox to let you out entirely.

Wynter: That's right. And they kept assigning me to pictures to be made abroad—like *The Lion* [1962] with Bill Holden, which was to be shot in Kenya—but I told them I couldn't take my two-year-old son there as the Mau-Mau atrocities were still going on—there was no way I'd risk that! So I was suspended for the duration of the filming. Also it rained so that it was held-up forever! *No Down Payment* [1957] was another assignment and I couldn't understand why anyone would be bothering to make that picture. "It's the most boring thing—life in a dreary housing development, for God's sake?! Absolutely not." So one way and another I spent a good deal of time without the salary. Those seven-year contracts were solely up to the studios to renew—yearly—or not. I think it was Olivia de Haviland who brought automatic extensions to an end when she took Jack Warner to court and the ruling was across the board: "No contract may last longer than seven years without re-negotiation by both participants." She claimed he was being spiteful by assigning her to rubbishy films he knew she'd refuse to keep her tied to Warner's indefinitely. "Slavery" might have been mentioned in the ruling. I was at Fox for seven years and could do nothing about it.

Weaver: What brought you to Ireland?

Wynter: They were to make *Shake Hands with the Devil* [1959] there and Fox sent me over. I'd never been to Ireland before and made a lot of Irish friends. I went back when John Huston wanted me for *The List of Adrian Messenger* [1963]—I played his own son Tony's mother. I had to ride in fox-hunting sequences, never having ridden sidesaddle before, and to drive a Land Rover. Oddly no-one bothered to discover whether I could do either of those things. But that was John Huston for you; one did what was expected. I bought the land in County Wicklow in

1966, a ruin composed of one chimney, and built a lovely stone house with a thatched roof. But since my son was still at school, I stayed in America until he was old enough to drive a car and go to university. That's when I started spending more and more time here. I love it but the winters are pretty hard, long and damp and grey. We were snowed in twice this year.

Weaver: So what's the best movie you were in?

Wynter: I was lucky to work with some very fine actors so its hard to   come up with a "best." *Playhouse 90's* were the highlight of my professional life. And the TV series *Twelve O'Clock High,* they wrote three tragic love-stories for me. But "entertainment" became too violent and scripts arrived which were uglier and uglier. The day came when I was playing another murderer, and a light went on in my head. "Here I am, a grown woman with a gun in her hand, and this is supposed to be *entertainment?* What am I doing here?" And after that show I quit. Grew up. Turned to journalism and have lived happily ever after. So to get back to your question, the answer is that I can't tell you. There aren't any films I did anything astonishing *in* or *with.* I never read my reviews and publicity, just as I never see films or TV I've worked in. Once lived, once done—that's it. Onward.

DANA WYNTER FILMOGRAPHY

White Corridors (1951)
Lady Godiva Rides Again (1951)
The Woman's Angle (1952)
It Started in Paradise (1952)
The Crimson Pirate (1952)
Colonel March Investigates (1952)
The View from Pompey's Head (Secret Interlude) (1955)
Invasion of the Body Snatchers (1956)
D-Day, the Sixth of June (1956)
Something of Value (1957)
In Love and War (1958)
Fraulein (1958)
Shake Hands with the Devil (1959)
Sink the Bismarck! (1960)
On the Double (1961)
The List of Adrian Messenger (1963)
If He Hollers, Let Him Go! (1968)
Airport (1970)
Santee (1973)
Le Sauvage (Lovers Like Us) (1975)

Dana Wynter and Kevin McCarthy on the
run in Invasion of the Body Snatchers (1956)

PHILIP KAUFMAN'S SECOND INVASION

— — —

Anthony Timpone

Toying with a movie classic is always risky business. The Hollywood landscape is littered with bad remakes, from Dino De Laurentiis's ridiculous *King Kong* to the Sharon Stone washout *Diabolique*. Not surprisingly, when director Philip Kaufman accepted the challenge to helm an update of 1956's *Invasion of the Body Snatchers*, he admits that he feared he might be stepping on hallowed ground.

But Kaufman's 1978 revamp is one of the rare ones that works, mainly due to the approach that he, screenwriter W. D. Richter, and producer Robert H. Solo brought to the familiar material. The trio set out to make "another version" of the Jack Finney novel, instead of a slavish copy, with the main difference being switching the pod takeover from small burg Santa Mira to major metropolis San Francisco. Kaufman took a "more organic" stab at the story and deftly orchestrated a "symphony of terror" that combined unsettling music, film noirish photography, and creepy sound effects to entrap the audience in a total paranoiac experience.

Born in Chicago in 1936 and educated at the University of Chicago and Harvard Law School, Kaufman taught for a while in Europe before returning to the States to begin work as an independent filmmaker in the sixties. His seventies films *The Great Northfield, Minnesota Raid* and *White Dawn* eventually caught the attention of producer Solo, who hired Kaufman for *Invasion*. Since then, Kaufman has emerged as one of the American cinema's true mavericks, winning praise for such films as *The Wanderers* (1979) and Best Picture Oscar nominee *The Right Stuff* (1983), as well as his two erotic epics, *The Unbearable Lightness of Being* (1988) and *Henry and June* (1990). In addition, Kaufman shared a story credit with buddy George Lucas on the 1981 Steven Spielberg blockbuster *Raiders of the Lost Ark*. Though he may not be the most prolific person working in films today (his last effort was 1993's *Rising Sun*), he is certainly one of the most talented. "I try to make movies that interest me deeply," Kaufman says. *Invasion of the Body Snatchers* was no exception.

Anthony Timpone: What first attracted you to remaking *Invasion of the Body Snatchers?*

Philip Kaufman: To some degree, I really didn't look on it as a remake. I looked on it as just another variation of the original theme. If we were going to remake it, we would have done the same story in the same small town and with the same approach. So it was [a question of] how to take that theme and do some variation of it. To some degree I felt the original, which I loved, was more connected almost with the world of slightly film noir, but almost a radio show where everything was narrated and everything was laid out with a certain kind of tension. I felt we could come up with something that was maybe a little more contemporary and visual, and bring the film into a larger city from that small-town atmosphere. It made it more relevant to the time in which it was made, in the seventies.

Timpone: Besides the novel and '56 film, were you inspired by any other sci-fi or horror films?

Kaufman: Not really. I would say that I was really more interested in the theme of paranoia, more of the Kafkaesque thing, which I felt was told really well both in the [1956] film and the Jack Finney book. Of people lost in a world where all of a sudden everything becomes, and all their feelings are of, paranoia, and yet it's not paranoia at all, because it's true [laughs]. So we made it clear from the very beginning that it was a science fiction film, as opposed to the Don Siegel version, by beginning on another planet. It was really meant to be the feelings you could feel around San Francisco at that time, with really believable characters.

Timpone: Didn't you screen 1933's *Island of the Lost Souls* beforehand?

Kaufman: Well, for visual reasons, but not for content, really. It was for the camera work and for how to get a film noir look into color, which you still don't see very much of. Going back to that time, some twenty years or so now, color just never seemed to have that same shadowy look, and that's what [cinematographer] Mike Chapman and I were trying to get.

Timpone: What made you go for a film noir look?

Kaufman: Because it had a creepy quality to it, and I felt most horror movies were almost lit like comedies in a strange way, and they weren't given, in most cases, the kind of treatment that they really deserved visually. They tended to get a kind of campy quality, because the lighting wasn't as powerful and as focused as it should have been. The great thing about film noir was that it really focused your eye right on what the filmmaker wanted you to focus on, and the shadows really kind of became characters in the piece.

Timpone: Unlike the first film and book, the audience seems to be one step ahead of the characters in your film. Why was that approach taken, where you know right from the start something "alien" is occurring?

Kaufman: Well, that was really to establish the fact that this was a science fiction movie right from the beginning, where you know that something strange was happening here. And to some degree the book has more of that quality; you do feel a little more of that sense of wonder more than the [1956] film, in a way. Jack Finney dealt more with the science fiction aspects than Don Siegel did, and we just pushed it that way, so that we could see our characters reacting to something that was... in fact, it became scarier to know, as I

Kevin McCarthy from The Invasion
of the Body Snatchers (1978)

said earlier, that their paranoia was not paranoia at all, but was in fact something really true. Whereas Don Siegel's film, which was great, partly because it was dealing with that time where one of the possible metaphors was the communist menace or something, people in an ordinary society were dealing with other people changing what seemed to be their political beliefs.

Timpone: As a director, it seems you were more comfortable with the psychological terror of the story than the action sequences, especially in the warehouse climax. Would you agree with that?

Kaufman: No. I'm a little surprised by that question, because I thought that the action and the effects were very well done for that time. I thought that the warehouse was a good climax, given the fact that the film was made for around $3.4 million. It was a big all-out pod central and got its just due. And there was as much action as we could put in; the running through the streets and all of that I felt was done in an exciting way. I like to do things like that.

Timpone: What kind of collaboration did you have with screenwriter W. D. Richter?

Kaufman: Well, we worked right from the beginning together and all the way through. He was off and on the set, and I talked to him quite a bit about what was going on, and if I had any new ideas I would call him and say,

"Look we want to do this and that, what can you do, how can we help?" The film was very collaborative, it was a lot of fun to make, because to some degree I viewed it, we all viewed it, as a comedy in a strange way, even though it's about scary things. For us it was partly because of the quality of the actors we used. There was always something funny underneath the surface. When you had Jeff Goldblum playing Bellicec, as opposed to the Don Siegel version, where the characters were super-serious about everything, Goldblum's character was quirky and odd, and someone you could laugh at and laugh with. And all the things Donald Sutherland, who is also a very funny guy, brought to the piece. There was a playfulness that all of us had in the making of it. I'm sure it was a very memorable time for everyone. The film was made pretty quickly, efficiently, and with high spirits.

Timpone: Which elements did you add to the script?

Kaufman: I don't know specifically all the changes. The ending, certainly, which we didn't tell anybody.

Timpone: The ending was your idea?

Kaufman: Yeah, we didn't tell that to anybody. I mentioned it to Richter, how I thought it should end, and then we talked to Solo. We never told the studio, so the studio never knew how it was going to end until they saw the movie. And I told Donald Sutherland either the night before or that morning, and if he hadn't bought into it we might have had some problems. But it seemed like the only possible conclusion, particularly working off the idea that Don Siegel's original film had been given the bookends that made it seem like all the danger was gone away, and it kind of sanitized the paranoia. Don had told me that that was a studio thing, and they had some comedy in the original, but that was taken out. I had known Don for a number of years, and we were friends, and even Kevin McCarthy talked to me about all the things that were taken out. Richter actually had set the first draft in a small town, and then I just felt no, this was a thing where we wanted to in a way show how that same story would have played out twenty years later and in a big city. In other words, if the virus had spread to a big city, how would you take the same theme and play it out over again, even though some of the characters have the same names, more or less? The idea was to do a variation on the theme of Don Siegel's thing rather than a straight remake of it. So there were many things I came up with, many things Richter came up with.

Timpone: Solo says you chose San Francisco because you lived there. Were there any other reasons?

Kaufman: Well, I think San Francisco was the perfect place for the thing, for all of those characters. The idea was that in a way it would be more scary if it were a liberal society rather than a conservative military society or something, that it could happen to people who were like Leonard Nimoy's character, for example. His psychoanalytic jargon made you think everything was all right all the time, and in fact there's something deeply wrong going on, and that's another reason why we wanted to have the science fiction stuff more clearly put in there. So that the audience could have more perspective on the psychoanalytic jargon that the psychiatrist in his Birkenstock sandals was using, especially when Leonard Nimoy finally turns around and we discover to our terror, our horror, that he's on the other side.

Timpone: What do you remember about shooting the effects scenes in the film?

Kaufman: Well, we shot them; it wasn't stuff that you go in for now with computer-generated images, it was all done right there in backyards of San Francisco at night; that is to say, the pods were growing into their final stage, and it was all done in live action. I remember the opening stuff on another planet, which I had a lot of fun with, the gelatinous material. I looked all over the city and we couldn't figure out how to do that, and somewhere in an art store I found this gel, which we paid about three dollars for. By putting it in water and reversing the camera movements and so forth, we were able to create the effect of another planet, and the opening effects scene probably cost us fifty bucks or something like that [laughs]. That was a lot of fun to do. I like to do effects that have the old-time jerry-rigged quality to them, rather than the super multimillion-dollar effects. Unfortunately, that was covered over with credits at the beginning, to my regret. I don't remember how that happened, exactly. Somebody was trying to shorten the movie by three minutes rather than leaving that alone and putting credits elsewhere. Those effects of the spores or whatever they are drifting through space would obviously have been much more powerful without the credits.

Timpone: What was it like directing your pal, Don Siegel? I read that he was very nervous.

Kaufman: He was as nervous as any director who isn't an actor would be. He really hadn't done that before, and he just came up here and suddenly was asking all the questions a director hates to be asked [laughs]: "Why am I doing this?" But once he got into it he was great, and he really had fun doing it, working with the crew in a way that he didn't have to be responsible for every shot, every move; he was terrific. He was a tough, hardened guy and suddenly he had to be kind of vulnerable. But that was the homage to Don Siegel. The whole film in a way was meant to be a homage to his version, which I respected so much. I was honored by his presence, and in turn was giving him back the film as a homage.

You've probably heard that story with Kevin McCarthy, it has been printed in a couple of places, where Kevin and I were shooting in the San Francisco Tenderloin, the scene where he finally runs into the car and is killed. He's shouting the same things that he was shouting at the end of the first film: "They're here, they're here!" And he's being chased by the crowd and it's as if he's run twenty years from the first movie all across the landscape from a small town into a big city to try and warn us, and he's about to warn Donald Sutherland. He bumps into the car and Donald's in the middle of telling this joke, and we never really get the punch line of the joke. He's killed, and as we were shooting the film, we did a number of takes with Kevin bumping into the car. The Tenderloin, if you know San Francisco, is kind of a Bowery area, a down-and-out area. It was a sensitive area in which to shoot, so there were a lot of street people around there, a lot of cult players. There was this one guy who took off all his clothes, and he was lying there with his head on the curb watching us shoot, and you couldn't tell these people to move because it would be politically incorrect and cause a lot of trouble. This guy called us over and he said to Kevin, "Hey, wasn't you in the first one?" And Kevin said, "Yeah, I was," and the guy said, "That was the better of the two" [laughs]. It was like we were getting our first review. Here we are just shooting the second one, and the guy is already giving the review [laughs]! Kevin fell down laughing.

Do you remember that joke Donald Sutherland was telling, do you know how it finishes?

Timpone: No.

Kaufman: The joke goes, the British are in the desert surrounded by Rommel, and he brings all his men together and says, "Listen, there's good news and there's bad news." (At that point Brooke Adams said, "I heard this one.") "The bad news is we've got nothing to eat but camel shit. The good news is there's plenty of it" [laughs].

Timpone: What did Siegel think of the completed film?

Kaufman: He really liked it. In fact, he said wonderful things. I don't really remember exactly, but he was a really big booster of the whole project and his presence helped everyone. We all loved working with him.

Timpone: Besides the obvious (the relationship between Miles/Donald Sutherland and Elisabeth/Brooke Adams), could you explain why you saw the film as a "tragic love story?"

Kaufman: Well, in a way it's a group of people, all of

whom are in love with each other. Donald sort of loves Jeff Goldblum, and Jeff Goldblum and Veronica Cartwright have their love story. I felt the problem we had in the movie was making the characters as human as possible, and that's where the humor came into it, like in the backyard where Brooke Adams rolls her eyes around. I discovered she could do this amazing thing where she can not only roll her eyes, but she can roll each one in the opposite direction. There's something so human about Donald Sutherland cooking Chinese food, and just the feelings that they all had for each other. So if you establish that humanity, then the loss of that humanity becomes that much more tragic. It wasn't just some cardboard characters that you sort of liked, or the people that were branded as your heroes suddenly became monsters; it was that when Jeff Goldblum became a pod, he was no longer that human being that you loved. However hurt and paranoid he was as a poet, you loved him. And Brooke Adams, she totally loses this great quality that she has in the movie. That's where the real tragedy lies. So in the film, we really tried to work on that tragic dimension.

Timpone: While shooting the film, you occasionally had to shut down production to discuss metaphysical pod problems. What were some of those discussions like?

Kaufman: I remember particularly one time when we

were shooting, my friend George Lucas had come to visit me on the set just at the time when Donald Sutherland didn't see how he would play one of his scenes a certain way. So we went into a room, and George sat outside for about two hours and then finally left. Donald was just going through some metaphysical anguish about how to play the scene. But fortunately, all the other actors felt, as Leonard Nimoy said, "I know my rôle and my character, so that no matter what Donald wants to do, I'm fine because I know how I'll react to anything he does." After discussing it, the actors and myself all worked out how we would approach the scene, and for Donald, suddenly something clicked in for him. It's one of the problems that you have when you don't have enough rehearsal time; he arrived at a scene and suddenly Donald didn't feel it made enough sense. He's an incredibly bright, sensitive actor, so we just wanted to make sure that the pod, prepod and postpod characters were in place for everybody.

Timpone: What led you to hire a Marin County psychiatrist, Denny Zeitlin, to do your score?

Kaufman: First of all, I've known him from college days. He was a wonderful jazz musician, and I just felt he would have some insight into paranoia. In discussing this with him, he got very enthusiastic about it, and we went over different types of music that I thought would be interesting, including Bernard

Herrmann and various other composers.
Denny sat with us and sat with it and really
worked hard and came up with a unique
and great score to the film. He said he never
wanted to do another score because it was
such hard work and took so much time out
of his practice, but the idea of having a psychiatrist, an expert in the loss of self and
paranoia, doing the score, seemed to me
exciting.

Timpone: Could you explain how you attempted to
exploit urban paranoia in the film and why
that theme appealed to you?

Kaufman: It has to do with neighborhoods, the lighting in neighborhoods, the lurking feeling
that there's always something dangerous
around the corner. Other science fiction
movies deal with this kind of thing, that
there is something scary in the world and
you just can't explain it away. It is there, and
there is the potential for something fearful,
and to some degree that's why people go to
horror or science fiction movies. It's because
they have inklings, things that cannot be
logically explained, that there is a terror
lurking. I think anybody who walks through
the city, particularly late at night, learns to
walk in a kind of guarded way, and you're
silly if you don't.

Timpone: Do you think the pop psychology elements
date the film today?

Kaufman: No, I think that same psychology is around

and in some ways is even more popular; it has spread even more. In a way, San Francisco was the avant-garde of that at the time, but now it has spread even more over the whole society more than it was then. So people who see the film now still seem to enjoy it.

Timpone: Were there any other themes that you hoped to explore in the film?

Kaufman: I was pretty happy with what it was, and the way we made it.

Timpone: In what way did Michael Chapman light the pod people to offer subtle visual clues to their nature?

Kaufman: Chapman is a great cinematographer, and I talked about all different ways of lighting it, and I don't remember the codes exactly that we worked out, but we had stages of pod-dom that were lit in a certain way. When someone really became a pod, it was a much more low-angle lighting on their faces. There were even some tints of color that we put to color them a little greenish around the gills. There were also those shadows, like when they're running away from the pods, the whole group, and you see all these huge shadows suddenly growing up on the wall. The shadows become another character in the piece. Using color almost in a way that color hadn't been used much before, because in color films, particularly Technicolor films, the idea was to get all the color you could get into a film, and here we were trying to take out as much color and only put in certain colors that we wanted there. Certainly Gordon Willis did that kind of stuff in the first *Godfather*, and Chapman was actually the [camera] operator on *Godfather*. But when you go back to the early seventies, that was something that hadn't been played around with as much. And we really didn't use a lot of long lenses to give it that smoky thing, we were using short lenses and trying to get crisp colors, and I don't think we even used a lens over seventy-five millimeters.

Timpone: Could you discuss the importance of sound in the film?

Kaufman: The sound was a big push for a long time. Dolby said it was the best soundtrack that they had, and they still use it for demonstrations of the use of Dolby. We really wanted to get that sense of the use of surround sound, the low rumbling. For example, when Don Siegel is riding through that tunnel and the motorcycles go by, being pursued, there were things that we did that really hadn't been done before, where the sound goes from rear screen where you see the motorcycles into speakers on the side and into the surrounds so that you really got the full effect, if you saw it in the right theater. You might not get that at home unless you have a surround system with a laser disc or something. That's the problem, unless the theater is really equipped for Dolby surround and the speakers are tweaked properly, which often doesn't happen. Now it has become more commonplace, but then we were pushing. By that I mean to say of all the people who did sound effects, the San Francisco people were very much in the avant-garde of sound effects at the time. For the mixer, Mark Berger, it was one of the first movies that he mixed. He's mixed hundreds since then. But we were trying to push the envelope a bit on the use of Dolby.

Timpone: In the seventies era of feel-good science fiction films like *Star Wars, Close Encounters of the Third Kind,* and *Superman,* do you think audiences weren't ready for a downbeat SF picture like yours?

Kaufman: Well, the film did very well, considering what it was. I think it would have done better had the release pattern been more of a modern release pattern, which hadn't been perfected then. In fact, I think it went into four hundred theaters and never went wider. Now it could have gone into two thousand theaters and then be much more widely seen. It had basically really good if not great reviews and pretty full houses everywhere it played, and was tremendously profitable given what it made. But it was released about Christmastime, and was up against a lot of big movies, like *Superman,* which came out the same time. Some of those movies were in much wider release, so there was a problem with what theaters we

	could get and so forth, and it was released in that transitional time, before modern release patterns were perfected.
Timpone:	Was the film tested in front of an audience?
Kaufman:	I think it was. I was busy making *The Wanderers*. Bob Solo took it around and tested it in a lot of places. I remember him calling me from Chicago, and the screenings were all good.
Timpone:	And United Artists' reactions were the same?
Kaufman:	Yeah, the studio was great. Once they saw it, they really liked it.
Timpone:	Were you aware of some of the film's ratings problems in Dallas and the subsequent lawsuit?
Kaufman:	No, I never heard that.
Timpone:	The local Dallas ratings board ruled that children under sixteen could not see *Invasion of the Body Snatchers* without a parent or guardian, thus challenging the MPAA's own PG label for the film. UA [United Artists] sued the city.
Kaufman:	No, I never heard that. I've had my own share of ratings problems, so that's interesting.
Timpone:	*Invasion* was your only major attempt at science fiction, before or after. Why?
Kaufman:	I don't know. I love to do sci-fi, and I was going to do the original *Star Trek*. That's

where I met Leonard, and really cast him, because I was building a whole script for *Star Trek* around Leonard Nimoy, around the Spock character, and I just wanted to work with him. I thought he was a wonderful actor, and I love science fiction and would love to do it [again]. I've tried to do a couple of things but nothing's come to fruition, and if you have anything that you think would make a great movie, send it to me immediately [laughs].

Timpone: Looking back on *Invasion of the Body Snatchers,* is there anything you would do differently?

Kaufman: No. I never really look back at my stuff, and I thought that it was fine at the time, and I never view [any] film again really. I've seen it fifty or five hundred times or however many times while I'm making it, I go through it over and over and over. And then once it is released, I never look at it again, and that's that, it is what it is.

AN INTERVIEW WITH W. D. RICHTER

— — —

Matthew R. Bradley

Quite literally a child of the postwar era, screenwriter W. D. "Rick" Richter was born in New Britain, Connecticut, on December 7, 1945, four years to the day after the bombing of Pearl Harbor and just months after the end of World War II, and educated at Dartmouth College and at U.S.C. Film School in Los Angeles. It is perhaps appropriate, then, that it fell to this lifelong genre enthusiast to reenvision, at times radically, such classics as *Invasion of the Body Snatchers* and *Dracula* for a new generation of filmgoers in high-profile remakes made during the late 1970s. The 1980s brought both an Academy Award nomination for the fact-based prison drama *Brubaker* and Richter's directorial debut with the cult favorite *The Adventures of Buckaroo Banzai Across the 8th Dimension,* starring such up-and-coming actors as Peter Weller, Ellen Barkin, and Jeff Goldblum. More recently, Richter has returned to the director's chair with the offbeat romantic comedy *Late for Dinner,* adapted Stephen King's bestseller *Needful Things* to the screen, and written the screenplay for *Home for the Holidays,* directed by actress Jodie Foster.

Matthew R.
Bradley: *Invasion of the Body Snatchers* (1978) seems like quite a switch from your earlier comedic credits on *Slither* (1973), *Peeper* (a.k.a. *Fat Chance*, 1975), and *Nickelodeon* (1976). What prompted your entry into the fantasy film genre?

W. D. Richter: When I was a kid, I liked horror and science fiction films as much as I liked anything. I actually probably watched them a little more religiously. I'd go to the movies by myself to see *The Day of the Triffids* [1963] and *The Blob* [1958] and all that stuff. It's just a wonderful release of the human imagination. I think that's its ultimate appeal: it takes you somewhere out there and makes you picture a universe that's just far more fantastic than the little town you're living in, or whatever your particular arena is at that time. So always in the back of my head was a sense of the magic of thinking about other worlds. I was a fan of that type of film, and then somebody comes along and for whatever reason gives you a chance to play around with one of them that you've really enjoyed all these years. I think the question might be, why did [producer] Bob Solo come to me? I guess he just liked the way I wrote, and maybe saw something in the eccentricity of some of it, I really don't know, but it was a delight to get the call, and I didn't have to hesitate.

Bradley: Did you work primarily from Jack Finney's

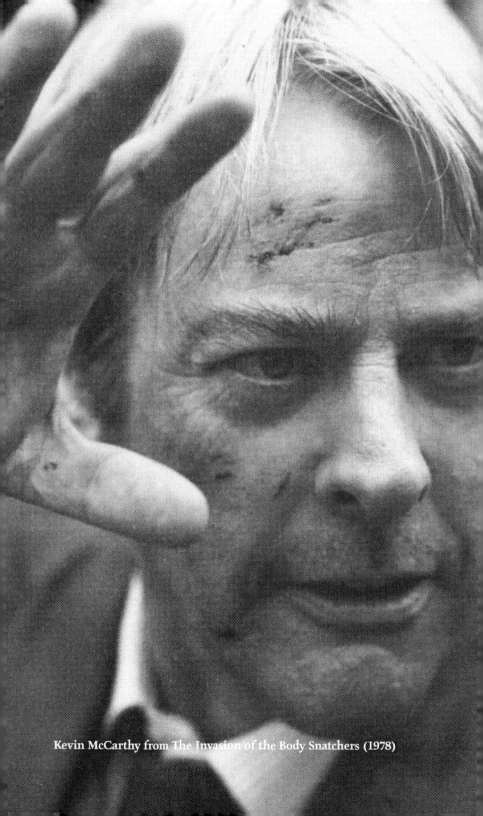

Kevin McCarthy from The Invasion of the Body Snatchers (1978)

novel *The Body Snatchers,* which was serialized in *Collier's,* or from Daniel Mainwaring's
earlier screenplay?

Richter: The Mainwaring script could never be
found—it was an enormous frustration to
all of us—so we had basically the novel and
the movie to work from. I'd say equally from
both. I certainly read the novel very care-
fully, and the biggest, most dramatic part of
that development process is that the first
incarnation of our version was also set in a
small town—contemporary, but a small
town. Now, Phil Kaufman had already
accepted from Bob Solo the job of developing
the material, and Bob called me without
telling me Phil was on it. I'd known Phil
casually through Ronda Gomez, who's a very
successful agent now and recently married
Howard Zieff, the director of *Slither.* After I
said, "Yes, I'd like to do it," Bob said, "Oh,
great, now we can all sit down with Phil and
we can start working on this." I said, "Who's
Phil?" "Phil Kaufman, didn't I tell you? He's
going to direct it." I said, "Bob, thank God I
like Phil. What if you had told me somebody
that I was uncomfortable with?" He said,
"Oh, I thought I mentioned it." We had a
delightful process of development, but
everybody's first instinct, without much
analysis, was, "It's enough to make it contemporary." Phil lived in the San Francisco
area, and we'd settled on shooting in the
outlying communities. So we were looking

at all sorts of small towns around San Francisco, trying to get the feel of what that
meant, like orchid houses out there that they
might be hidden in and stuff. That was the
draft that I wrote, and that's the draft that
Mike Medavoy gave the green light to. We
were in preproduction, and I don't remember how far in, I think about seven or eight
weeks from the start of principal photography. Phil and I were talking one day in the
office, and he was, I think, losing confidence
in the concept of making a small-town film.
It came out of this conversation that maybe
we'd miscalculated, and that it was more
interesting to locate the paranoia in a large
city—that it might be easier for them to
hide, and that that would be a more ener-
gized version of it. If long ago we thought
the communists were taking over the heart
of America, our small towns, then if we had
fears today it had more to do with how we
were losing the center of our civilization,
because our cities were starting to seem
strange. They weren't necessarily representa-
tive of the best of us, but maybe the worst of
us. So Phil and I said to each other, "We have
made a mistake here. What if we set in a big
city? Are we being crazy?" We talked for a
little bit and decided that the narrative we'd
come up with wouldn't be that radically different. People's occupations would change,
but the essential plot moves might not be
that different. He said, "How on Earth can
we tell Medavoy this?" Well, we just got up

out of the office, and I can picture the two of us as if I'm a fly on the wall, watching these two guys go down the hall. He said, "We have to be really good in this room." Mike was very sympathetic. He heard the new version of it, and he said, "You guys are right. I mean, I wish you'd thought about it a year ago, but what will it take? Can you do it, Phil?" He trusts filmmakers, that's the wonderful thing about Mike Medavoy. Phil said, "We will do it. Rick will be there every minute. We will locate it very quickly for logistical purposes in San Francisco." It didn't take long to come up with notions of mud baths and things like that, but to get the dialogue more urban, et cetera, I was going to have to be writing during the whole production, which I did. I stayed in San Francisco, and I finished well before they were through with principal photography, but I'm sure I was doing rewrites during the whole movie. I was there all the time. I saw all the dailies, I was on the set an awful lot, but a lot of times I was in the hotel writing. It was an exciting thing to be doing, because we all felt we were really making a film that we believed in, and had had the nerve to change our minds at the last minute and try to make it better, and had the total support of the studio [United Artists] to do that. I think that was a time when films were made perhaps a little more on content than on release dates. The target was to get a good film rather than to get it

out in August, although we had to go right
away, not because of a release date but
because so many people had been put on
who were working. Mike Medavoy said, "If I
shut everything down, I'm going to have to
pay all these people off," and we said, "You
don't have to. We're trying to be mindful of
costs." I think the movie cost $3 million or
something, and we thought we owed everybody. Staying on the original schedule
seemed to be our responsibility at that point.
It was fun, kind of guerrilla filmmaking.

Bradley: Like yourself, Kaufman is both a screenwriter and a director. Did he work with you
on actually writing the screenplay, or just
conceptualizing?

Richter: Just conceptualizing. He functioned completely as a director developing a piece of
material.

Bradley: In terms of resetting the story in a major
city, Phil Hardy's *Overlook Film Encyclopedia*
states that you and Kaufman "wittily update
[it] by replacing the simple contrast
between rational 'pod' people and emotional
humans with the more complex idea that
urban alienation makes it virtually impossible to distinguish between pods and people."
Was that in fact your intention?

Richter: Absolutely. I think that what the film is
about on some level is not how something
can take over the person closest to us, but
how we're all so complex, that we have

many facets that we reveal. Never mind do we ever really know ourselves, but do we ever really know the person we're living with, having a conversation with, working with? It's just a chilling fact of life to me. It's not so much urban alienation but the human condition, that we are very complex. We are playacting a lot of times to do the right thing in a given situation, and construct a personality that's full of layers, and you may not really understand the person that you're putting in an awful lot of time with. I don't want to say that that was something I was aware of in every scene, because we were really trying to write something that was spirited and moved on the surface as much as beneath it, but those are the things I was thinking about at the time. You're talking to somebody and you don't know if they're really listening but they're sure having a conversation with you.

Bradley: I presume that was why you added the character of the heroine's lover, Geoffrey, who has no analog in previous versions of the story?

Richter: Right, exactly.

Bradley: Were you daunted by following in the footsteps of the original film's director and star, Don Siegel and Kevin McCarthy, who both made cameos in yours?

Richter: No, because we respected their work, and they made it much the same way. They did-

n't sit down to create this timeless masterpiece, they had a good time making that
movie, and we were just trying to do the
same thing. It wasn't like it was a perfect
movie, and we thought we were doing
something different enough that we weren't
truly in their shadow. Also, certain people
would see our version who had never seen
theirs, unless you were a real serious film
fanatic. People don't necessarily get to see
the other, so we thought, "Well, we'll just do
the best we can here, and who knows
whether it'll be better or worse or just sort of
equal in a different way?"

Bradley: Was the chance to use more sophisticated
effects an impetus for the remake?

Richter: I don't think so. I think this was a time
when we were still making movies about
human beings, and of course you knew
you'd have more resources, but it wasn't a
world that flew in special effects people and
other camera crews to do digital moves that
would later be added. There weren't experts,
so we all sat around and I watched production designers try to figure out how you
make a pod, what's inside it. That wasn't
sophisticated stuff, so it wasn't like, "Wow,
do we have the tools now." It was more like,
the story resonates, the themes can be
evocative, and wouldn't that be nice if that's
what was motivating films today? But no.
Now, we know what we can do, so therefore
we'll devise something that will demonstrate

our technical skills. We were still coming from the center of a movie, from the heart of it.

Bradley: Jeff Goldblum, who later appeared in Kaufman's *The Right Stuff* (1983) and your own *Adventures of Buckaroo Banzai Across the 8th Dimension* (1984), was quite effective in his supporting role. Did you sense a star in the making?

Richter: Not a star, because Jeff is a true wonderful eccentric, but certainly a presence that was not going to go away, and if he was handed proper roles would be an indelible mark on the American filmscape. I mean, he's just special. You know it when Jeff starts looking at you or talking to you, off camera or on, you just grin, because he's a wondrous creation. I love that he was in that movie, because he did things with it that you hope can happen.

Bradley: Wasn't that Robert Duvall as the priest on the swing in the first scene? I know he'd been in Kaufman's *The Great Northfield Minnesota Raid* (1972).

Richter: Yes. He was swinging on the swing as a priest, just to do that for Phil.

Bradley: I kept thinking maybe he would turn up later on as a pod priest.

Richter: See, that's the problem with those. You get all excited when you do them, but then you tend to forget that it's saying something to the audience, and it's misleading. It's truly misleading, because that's just Robert Duvall on a swing. That was just game-playing, and you have to be careful about that.

Bradley: And then you spend the rest of the movie wondering who else will pop up.

Richter: These are the buttons you're pushing that you don't think about, and as you get more experienced you say, "Oh, nice idea, but that's just going to be an indulgence, and cause slight little weird problems that'll send tremors through the audience that we're not trying to do."

Bradley: Was the strange hybrid of a street singer and his dog, produced by a damaged pod, inspired by the dog in a human mask from *The Mephisto Waltz* (1971)?

Richter: Boy, I don't know, because I know that movie. I used to kid around and call it *Rosemary's Piano.* So obviously, you know, if it's in there... I just don't remember whether we said, "Oh, that would be cool," or if we just thought of it. You couldn't get at films as easily as you can now, they weren't bouncing all over the airwaves, so unless Phil remembers, I would have no idea.

Bradley: The frequent references to conspiracy by the characters in the remake seem to suggest that the post-Watergate era provided just as fertile ground, if you'll excuse the pun, for this particular tale as the Cold War hysteria of the 1950s.

Richter: I'm sure it did, because it was part of our reflexive thinking at the time. We were just so convinced that everything was happening behind our backs that unconsciously, I suppose, you approach the creative process with that in the air, but I don't think there was any sense that that's why we were making this movie. We just thought it was a really good story, and it seemed to still have a reason for existing in the complicated world of the present tense at that time, but there wasn't any axe to grind. It wasn't like a new way to talk about conspiracy theories or anything.

Bradley: Though the invaders are driven off in Finney's novel, many have expressed dissatisfaction with the studio-imposed happy ending of Siegel's film, on which McCarthy's fate in the remake seems to be an ironic commentary. Was this a contributing factor in the decision to end yours on a downbeat note?

Richter: I suspect it was less political like that than it was just our feeling that that would be the most unsettling way to get to the audience, and I suppose express maybe that sense you brought up, that there were forces out there that were not going to go away, and you just might be overwhelmed by them. Maybe that's too cynical a thing to admit, but I think we were talking about it in the middle of that feeling that there were serious problems out there in the culture. The film is cer-

tainly not presenting a solution, but probably trying to reflect the danger of not being
aware of what's going on around you.

Bradley: I've noticed that each successive incarnation
of the story seems to grow darker in tone. In
the novel, for example, all of the main characters survive, while in Siegel's film Becky
and the Belicecs become pod people, and in
your version even Bennell loses his humanity. Is everything just going to hell?

Richter: Well, if you have a vast historical overview,
you say, "It was pretty difficult in the thir-
teenth century, and it wasn't a lot of fun in
the fifteenth," but we tend to watch the
progress of our own life spans. We can't help
it, I mean, that's what we're living through.
I'm a child of basically postwar America, and
it was pretty great when you first got a
sense of, "Oh, I live in America, and I make
snowmen, and run around in the summer."
It *has* gotten darker, or if not gotten darker
the darkness is seeping out into the light,
and we're aware that it's a much more dangerous, complicated, and threatening world
than it felt like to most people in, say, 1952.
I don't think the culture feels like it's on a
journey right now toward a new renais-
sance, so I suppose we're getting more and
more nervous with each passing year. No
matter what the stock market's doing, people
know down deep that it can't go on forever
and it's being motivated by screwy needs;
people have to protect themselves for a dark,

scary future by making as much money as they can, so that when a wolf comes to the door they'll be able to shoot it. So yeah, we're getting a creepy feeling that things are getting slightly worse if not better.

Bradley: And whereas in the fifties, despite the fifth columnists and Reds under the bed, the threat was mainly external, but in the seventies, with all the awareness of what our own government was doing, the threat was within.

Richter: Maybe if there's a point about the pod people, it's that they represent something that's right in front of us all the time, and we might not recognize it. You keep the metaphor that it came from somewhere else, but it seems to me that it's us. We'd better be very careful we don't turn into something that seems so alien from where we began that we're just destroying ourselves.

Bradley: How did you hit on the idea of the scream used by the pods to finger humans? It's certainly a key part of the effectiveness of the ending—it's devastating.

Richter: I don't remember. It's a very special sound, too. It has some of that African ululation, a tribal noise they make. We had endless hours of discussion about what the whole film should look and sound like. Mike Chapman is an extraordinary cinematographer, and we were trying to get such a weird edginess in. There are some passing shots in there that almost look like darker versions of Edward Hopper—an apartment building with somebody visible inside it, just sort of at a kitchen window or something, I recall. On the way back from locations, Michael was always shooting out of the windows of cars, trying to get textures of the city. We were listening to city noises, sirens and dump trucks, familiar sounds, so sound was always a very important part of this. Ben Burtt, who turned into one of George Lucas's major collaborators, did the sound in that film. I will always remember going to this little primitive room he had where he was creating the noises of the pods opening up. He had this delicate little microphone suspended off of an Lshaped bracket. It was, to my recollection, the size of a pencil eraser hanging four or five inches off the table top, and he was cracking zucchini and cucumbers and stuff. The sound design in that film was always essential to its working, so it's not a casual thing that you were unnerved by it.

Bradley: And I noticed that the cinematography creates so many unnerving, unsettling little moments where nothing significant is necessarily even taking place, but they combine to provide a cumulative sense of real unease and dread.

Richter: That's really nice to hear, and I love it when everybody's working together like that. There's a moment that comes to mind when they're all in Matthew's apartment, and Veronica Cartwright is into this speech about, "Why do we always expect aliens to come in metal ships?" There's a cutaway to Donald Sutherland as he's being deeply rattled by the depth of her confusion and fear, and he's standing on a dolly. The camera's stationary, and he is being moved just incrementally, but that's changing his relationship to the doorframe that he's in and the room behind him. That's a different effect than if you were creeping the camera, because only the frame would be moving. So Donald is actually moving inside the frame, and the background is not. The background and the camera are in the same universe, and Donald is sort of gliding through it, but at such a slow rate that you don't perceive it and say, "Why is that guy moving?", because the cut is so short. It's a very disconcerting image, because he's got a look on his face like his eyes are sort of screwed together and he's trying to figure it out. They've gotta know she's not talking bullshit here, and the shot has that internally. There's a slight sense of dizziness or light-headedness without it being shoved in your face. Probably a lot of people aren't even affected by it, and some are and don't know it's there, but those things are sprinkled throughout the movie, and that's really good storytelling, I think. It's also in another way an attempt, at least, to use the ordinary, like those red dump trucks. And even at the airport, there are these droning voices about, "the red zone is for loading and unloading," and then in that same cadence is some reference to pods in the same voices—"unload your pods," so you're hearing the ordinary and the extraordinary all mixed together in sort of numbing, almost muzak, public address stuff. Who knows what's penetrating the audience's sensibility? It's slyly funny and sinister all at once, and that's what we were trying to do.

Bradley: Strictly speaking, Abel Ferrara's *Body Snatchers* [1993] is neither a remake nor a sequel, but more a variation on a theme. What was your reaction to it?

Richter: I have not seen the film. However, I was sent the screenplay, and it had no acknowledgment of our movie, so I thought, "It's obviously based on the book." Bob Solo was one of the producers. Actually the reason I was sent the screenplay is because when the Writer's Guild gets a thing like that, they have a way of churning out of their database the fact that there were previous movies and other writers on them, and they're always protecting us. They say, "We noticed the producers are asking for a certain credit on it, so we're sending copies to the other writers," and in fact the scream was in there. I said, "Wait a minute—this is interesting, because this is a very subtle thing happening here." There were a handful of small things that I knew specifically did not come from the book, and we were into an extraordinarily dicey moment there. Warner Bros. made that movie and United Artists made ours, though I believe it was owned by MGM at the time, because the United Artists' library fell into MGM's lap when they took over the studio. I'm sitting here reading this script, thinking, "Not only are these things coming from my adaptation, but they are being, on a purely legal level—not that this is intentional—stolen by Warner Bros. from MGM, because MGM owns the rights to all the material that was created specifically for our film." So I spoke to Bob Solo about this and said, "You must have shown them that script," and he said, "Well, I guess they did see it." Whether it was sloppiness on their part or whatever, they didn't remember where certain things came from. There was a slight settlement on that. I don't know if the studios ever directly addressed each other, but I was given some compensation just to acknowledge the fact that they used some of my stuff. It's that basic. I've had literally no desire to see it. I saw the final shooting script. That's what the Guild is forced to show you.

Kevin McCarthy and Donald Sutherland from
The Invasion of the Body Snatchers (1978)

ROBERT H. SOLO, POD PRODUCER

— — —

Anthony Timpone

After author Jack Finney, director Don Siegel, and actor Kevin McCarthy, the person most associated with the *Body Snatchers* films is producer Robert H. Solo, who shepherded both the acclaimed 1978 version and the ill-fated 1994 adaptation to the screen.

Born in 1932 in Waterbury, Connecticut, Solo has produced numerous films during the last three decades, including *The Devils, Scrooge, Colors, Winter People, Above the Law,* and *Blue Sky.* A fan of the original movie since his youth, Solo dug into his own wallet to purchase the rights to Finney's *The Body Snatchers* in 1975, a few years before the George Lucas/Steven Spielberg-driven sci-fi boom of the late seventies.

For this former talent agent, studio executive, and independent producer, *Body Snatchers* represents the best of times and worst of times. The best: his association with director Philip Kaufman's chilling remake that starred Donald Sutherland and reset Finney's small-town story in San Francisco. The worst: Abel Ferrara's moderately effective update, relocated to a southern army base, which became a victim of studio politics. Now semiretired and living in Nevada, the veteran producer is quite proud of his

1978 *Invasion of the Body Snatchers*. However, Solo's attempt to relaunch Finney's trendsetter as a filmic franchise for the nineties left him questioning whether the pods had already invaded Hollywood.

Anthony
Timpone: When did you first see the '56 film?

Robert
H. Solo: Probably the year it came out or the year after, and it was terrific, it just scared the daylights out of me. I've seen it once or twice after that, and it just always stuck in my head as one of those movies that registers very powerfully on you, and so it was part of my repertoire of movies that I remember. It was no surprise when later on I was thinking about things to do and what subjects to make, and I thought of *Invasion of the Body Snatchers*.

Timpone: Had you read the book before you saw the movie?

Solo: No. No, I had not read the book, I didn't even know it was a book at that time. And obviously I read the book more than once in '75 or '76, when I first got the idea to do a movie on it.

Timpone: Why did you decide to remake a film that many consider a classic?

Solo: Well, first of all, I thought that it had an opportunity to be remade in color, not black and white. And compared to what they had in '56, I thought we could do a lot better in the special effects area. Of course, by today's standards, even our special effects are from the stone age! Those were really the main reasons, other than the fact that I always felt that the ending of the '56 version was a cop-out and a joke, and always made me laugh, actually. You know, "Call the FBI [laughs]," like they're going to save the world. That was ridiculous. Having read the novel, I thought that one could do what was in the novel or something that was akin to what was in the novel, but certainly not what was in the 1956 movie.

Timpone: What made you take the risk of plunking down $10,000 of your own money to grab the rights?

Solo: I don't know. It was something I really wanted to do, and the only way to do it was to get an option on it. I had an exclusive two-year producer deal at Warner Bros. and had been trying to find projects for about a year when I thought about this. I suggested it to them, and they didn't want to do it. I still had time to go on my contract and I thought, "Well, I really want to do this, and I want to try and put it together, and Warners isn't gonna put money up for me. I'll just have to do it myself." I didn't have all that much, but I reached in my pocket and I got an option.

Timpone: Warner Bros. eventually began developing the film. Why did they then put it in turn-around and decide to pass?

Solo: To this day I have no idea. I have no idea why they just finally did develop it and then put it in turnaround. By then I had a script and I had full confidence, so I can't imagine.

Timpone: Besides the '56 *Invasion,* were you a fan of other science fiction or horror films?

Solo: Well, not as a general rule, no. I like science fiction. I used to read science fiction and fantasy magazines in the forties or fifties, maybe when I was in high school. So I always liked science fiction, and I always like the old H. G. Wells movies. I was drawn to science fiction, but not as an aficionado or freak. I didn't go to conventions.

Timpone: Were any other scripters hired to work on the project besides W. D. Richter?

Solo: No, he was the only one.

Timpone: Wasn't the original intention to set the film in a small town and follow the Siegel film more closely?

Solo: That was the intention. The original intention was to do a 1978 remake, and originally it started out in the same small town as it was in the book and film. But that changed in the course of development. Actually, it changed while I was out of the room. We were sitting talking about the script and what we were doing, Richter and Phil Kaufman, and I went to the men's room, and I came back and they said, "We're moving it to San Francisco." I gasped and my eyes bulged out, and I thought about it and it was just such a wild idea, so I said, "Terrific, great, let's do that." So that's how it happened. I don't know who broached it, probably Phil because he lives in San Francisco. And as I know Phil better now over the years—I didn't really know him well then—he likes to live at home, so I guess he just wanted to go home every night [laughs]. So he said, "Let's make this happen in San Francisco."

Timpone: What led to the hiring of Kaufman? He was somewhat untried at that time.

Solo: Well, he had made a couple of movies, and I had seen *The Great Northfield, Minnesota Raid,* and *White Dawn,* and they struck me as being very cinematically unusual. They weren't conventional movies the way they were shot. There was something really interesting and offbeat and off-key about the way those films were made. So that attracted me to him. I didn't know him, so I called his agent, and at the time he was working on *Star Trek* [the first feature film attempt], which I hadn't known. And then somebody at Paramount canceled *Star Trek* because they thought there was no future in science fiction movies, and so he became available to do *Body Snatchers.* We always used to laugh about *Star Trek.*

Timpone: What did you contribute to the screenplay in those early days?

Solo: I have no idea. I presume something. I mean,

it's hard to keep my mouth shut. So I'm sure I made a contribution, but believe me, I couldn't tell you what it was.

Timpone: Let's talk about the casting of the film. What led to your ultimate choices: Donald Sutherland, Brooke Adams, Leonard Nimoy, Jeff Goldblum, and Veronica Cartwright?

Solo: I don't know. Jeff Goldblum and Veronica Cartwright came in as general casting. We had seen Brooke Adams in *Days of Heaven*. We needed to get some kind of a name in it for United Artists to go ahead with it, and someone said Donald Sutherland was back in the country. And he was an old client and friend of Mike Medavoy, United Artists' West Coast head of production. So between Mike and ourselves we approached Donald, and he agreed to do it, and everything keyed off of that. Of course, we didn't have much of a budget, and we had very little money for cast, and he got most of it. It was considerably lower than he had gotten in the past, but then he hadn't made an American picture in a long time. We didn't really have any money for anyone else, so all we could pay anybody else was $25,000. That's the most anybody got. That means Jeff Goldblum got $25,000, Brooke Adams got $25,000. I'm not sure Veronica got that, but the rest of the principals did. It was difficult to convince Leonard Nimoy to do the movie for $25,000; he had come off of *Star Trek* and was quite a name, but he did it for Phil, who got to know him while he was preparing *Star Trek*.

Timpone: So Sutherland was the first choice for the lead role?

Solo: When his name came up, we all said, "Gee, that's a great idea!" We wanted an actor who gave the appearance of being intelligent, somewhat aggressive, because he was going to be a health inspector who would go in and ask questions and be credible in that kind of occupation.

Timpone: How much was Sutherland paid?

Solo: Something between $200,000 and $300,000.

Timpone: It must have been a tough shoot: lots of locations, night scenes, not to mention the special effects.

Solo: Well, it was difficult because so much of it was at night. It was really exhausting for everybody, everybody except me, because I'd usually go home and go to bed at one o'clock or two in the morning. I'm an early person, so I'd be up at six-thirty or seven o'clock. But when it was night shooting, I couldn't handle it, having been up all day. It was very hard night after night after night, like out on the warehouse location where we shot the greenhouse where they were raising all the pods. It was right on the water, and it was very damp and cold. But compared to other locations I've been on, it was a picnic.

It wasn't that difficult to shoot. It was difficult to shoot it with the time and money we had, because we had a lot we had to do.

Timpone: What was your shooting schedule?

Solo: About ten weeks. I don't remember what the budget was, it was around $3 million dollars, 3.2 or something. But the city of San Francisco was very cooperative. And all in all I don't think it was a nightmarish shoot at all, by any stretch of imagination. I can't tell you any horror stories.

Timpone: Do you have any location anecdotes, like when you were shooting in the red-light district?

Solo: When we were shooting in the Market Street area, South of Market, there were lots of drunks around all the time. It was sort of like the Bowery, that kind of area. I guess they're cleaning it up and have reclaimed it today. But then it was still a lot of drunks and people yelling out in the middle of the take and all that business, chasing after Donald Sutherland and Leonard.

Timpone: Was the Jack Bellicec character conceived from the start as comic relief, or was that something that Jeff Goldblum improvised?

Solo: No, that's the way it was conceived, a kind of a New Age character spouting drivel. And as was Leonard Nimoy on the other side of it, it was all because it was right in the seventies when all that stuff was going on. EST was very popular, and all these self-improvement movements were at their height. Everyone was into some sort of a group looking for self-awareness and insight and so on. So we incorporated all that into the script, and it was in the temper of the times.

Timpone: What other themes, besides EST and the New Age philosophy, did you wish to explore?

Solo: Just urban paranoia.

Timpone: Is it true that you started filming without a completed script, and the actors didn't know the ending until late in the game?

Solo: Well, we had completed the script but the actors didn't know the ending, and neither did Donald Sutherland. And of course that was crucial, because he had to do it! We had been shooting out of sequence about three or four weeks, so the time came when we were down around downtown San Francisco, where all the office buildings are. We had been shooting with Donald and we had to shoot the end of the movie the next day. It was the next *day.* We didn't tell Donald, he didn't know about it. So Phil grabbed me and said, "Listen, we've gotta go tell Donald the end of this movie" [laughs]. And we went to his trailer, nervous I may say, and Don said, "Well, I've been expecting you" [laughs]. And then we told him what the ending of the movie was, and he thought it was terrific, and we were very relieved.

Timpone: Cartwright said that Sutherland was a bit of an eccentric, and showed up at a three-hour rehearsal with pink curlers in his hair.

Solo: Well, Donald is Donald. He flew in his own crazy hairdresser from New York and wanted to be in curls for some reason in the movie. God knows why he wanted to have curls. I don't remember [Cartwright's] situation, but I'm sure it was true [laughs]. And I think we toned it down a little bit, but he wanted to have curls. Of course, Donald has always been a little eccentric.

Timpone: Did Nimoy see his role as a career breakthrough?

Solo: Oh, I don't think so. He did it because he thought it would be fun; he certainly didn't do it for the money. It wasn't the lead in the movie, so it couldn't possibly be a career break. He did it for Phil and did it for fun.

Timpone: Did the four leads bond while you were shooting?

Solo: You mean personally?

Timpone: Yes, did they become a pretty tight-knit group?

Solo: Well, most of them, not all. Not all. I really don't want to go into where there was conflict, but there was.

Timpone: How did the uncredited Robert Duvall cameo come about?

Solo: He's a pal of Phil's, and he happened to be in San Francisco. So Phil grabbed him and said, "You're going to be in the movie, and I'm gonna make you a priest!" And I guess they had a priest costume on the wardrobe truck, and they put him on a swing. And that was it, just a spur-of-the-moment thing. Whereas Don Siegel was not a spur-of-the-moment thing.

Timpone: Was Duvall supposed to be the first pod person?

Solo: Yes, I think so. Yeah.

Timpone: Whose idea was it to cast Kevin McCarthy and Don Siegel?

Solo: It was all of our idea, because we all loved the [1956] movie, and so we thought it would be terrific to get them in. And Phil was a friend of Don Siegel, because they were both under contract to Universal. So we decided we'd make it a little bit of a homage to Don, and Phil called Don and asked him if he'd be in it. Don said he would love to, so that was easy. Kevin McCarthy loved the idea, but we started out with the equivalent of two dollars and ended up with two hundred dollars in order to get him. If you're going to get Kevin McCarthy you have to get Kevin McCarthy, you can't get anybody else. His agent kept asking for more and more, so we paid a lot of money, relatively speaking, for somebody to come out and work one day.

Timpone: How did Ben Burtt accomplish the legendary pod scream?

Solo: It's something playing backwards, a pig squealing or something like that.

Timpone: Whose decision was it to show more of the pods and their physiology, as compared to the first film?

Solo: Everybody's. We wanted to just make it more colorful and more graphic.

Timpone: Did the effects go off as planned, for the most part?

Solo: Yeah, for the most part. There were some problems with the pods and all that stuff in the beginning, but we worked it out, and of course today it would all be done in computers, and it would take a lot less time.

Timpone: Do you remember how the pod effects were accomplished?

Solo: Vaguely, only vaguely. I know that we dug a hole and we had some kind of a hydraulic thing that pushed the person up and it opened up.

Timpone: Was there a conscious decision to make the pod people more zombielike than in the '56 film? In the '78 film, they move more stiffly and deliberately.

Solo: A little bit. But you saw more of the pod people in the '78 version than you did in the '56 version. But on the one hand, some of them move slowly, and then at other times you have these dialogue scenes in the house with Leonard Nimoy, where he was just spouting his New Age philosophy to Jeff Goldblum, but he was a pod. And you didn't know that until the end of the scene when they go out and Nimoy says, "Tell somebody to go get them." You didn't know that he was a pod until the scene was over. So while we had some of them walking zombielike, it wasn't universal.

Timpone: Was George Romero's *Night of the Living Dead* used as a reference in any way?

Solo: I don't think so. It never came up at all.

Timpone: Was *The Exorcist* or any other film used as a model for an approach to adult horror while you were making the film?

Solo: I don't think so. I don't remember any of that ever coming up in any of our conversations. Phil wanted to screen some film noir for the lighting and stuff like that. Shadows, a lot of shadows and things like that. Just for visual reasons.

Timpone: Did you ever consult Jack Finney on the film?

Solo: No, he wasn't consulted. And he got a little pissed off at me, at us really. He and his agent were pissed off in the first place because we didn't pay him. We didn't *have* to pay him. We got the rights from the people who owned the rights to the book, and to the old movie. So when we wanted to do a remake, we got the rights from those people. And I think he and his agent were upset that he wasn't getting more money, which of course never happens. When someone buys the rights to a book, they own the book. If they want to sell it to somebody else, they sell it to somebody else, and he was not thrilled. By the time we were in San Francisco, Finney was quite annoyed, and then we belatedly invited him down to be in that book party scene with Leonard Nimoy, and he refused to come. So that was our association with him.

Timpone: Did you rekindle your association when it came time to do the nineties version?

Solo: No, it was just a lost cause by that point. What was the point?

Timpone: Were any other endings discussed for the '78 remake?

Solo: Well, there was the ending that was in the book, which was never shot, where they pour oil in the furrows in the field and set fire to it, and it burns up all the pods. They start burning and popping off the vines and then float up into the atmosphere, as if perhaps they're going to end up on some other planet somewhere. And the pod people that were already here had no future, because they weren't going to be succeeded by any future pod people without the pods. So that was the book. We had talked about that, or some variations on that.

Timpone: Do you think the film still holds up today?

Solo: I think so. I think the '56 film holds up, for the most part. And ours holds up, too. Of course, it was a reflection of the time, of 1978, what attitudes were, how people behaved, what kind of clothes they wore and the normal gobbledygook. But it's a very modern film and has done pretty well on video, and continues to do very well, so it's not on the dust heap of history.

Timpone: Do you think the film would have been more successful if it had ended more upbeat?

Solo: Of course; any film is going to be more successful if it ends upbeat, any film. Studios hate downbeat movies, and audiences don't want to walk out of the theaters grim, they want to walk out with at least a feeling of hope. Audiences like pictures to end on a positive note, whether it's brimming with enthusiasm or whatever, but not a negative note. Movies that end on a negative note usually flop. So that was the risk that we took, and of course we paid for it, because the movie was not a big hit. And we opened the same day as Clint Eastwood in *Every Which Way But Loose,* and it just killed us.

Timpone: The movie pulled in about $12 million in rentals.

Solo: Yeah, maybe ten or twelve. And it became a very profitable movie for its cost, because they sold it to network television. It was one

148

of the last big sales to network TV; they sold it for something like $6.5 million to one of the networks for three or four showings. And then of course it has always had a pretty good life on video. So the movie was a profitable one, there was no question. It was sort of thrown away foreign because all those people that we had done business with at United Artists had left the company by then.

Timpone:　What was your involvement in the proposed *Body Snatchers* TV series?

Solo:　I had nothing to do with it; as a matter of fact, I don't think there will ever be a *Body Snatchers* TV show, because there's a problem with the rights. When I made the 1978 version I got the rights, and when I made the deal with United Artists I didn't have them all, but I had to give them rights to a television series, and the rights to a television series were frozen between them and me. In other words, they weren't really in the television business, so they couldn't make a series without me and I couldn't make a series without them. So then when I made the deal with Warner Bros., they took over my rights, so now Warner Bros. can't make the series without United Artists, United Artists can't make the series without Warner Bros. So the likelihood of that ever happening is slim. But seven or eight years ago, United Artists started developing a television series without even telling me, based on the movie. So I gather they got a script, tried to shop it, and couldn't sell it. Of course, they had no right to do it without me and there would have been a major lawsuit.

Timpone: Do you know what that series would have been like?

Solo: I have no idea, I never saw it.

Timpone: At what time did you decide to try the formula again and do another *Body Snatchers* movie?

Solo: Well, I thought that there was a way to do it that would be totally different—and of course it didn't turn out that way—but it would be totally different. My idea was that initially it was set in a small town in the Midwest, and nearby was an air base, and so basically they're taking over the air base, and from that the pods were going to take over the country through the military. So in a way it was going to be a kind of revolution, and it was going to be a military regime. That was the original idea.

Timpone: Was Raymond Cistheri hired by you to work on the *Body Snatchers* script?

Solo: Who?

Timpone: Raymond Cistheri is credited for the story with Larry Cohen.

Solo: Oh, yeah. I tell you, I don't want to go into the writing credits on this movie.

Timpone: Too complicated?

Solo: Yeah, too complicated.

Timpone: So then you probably wouldn't want to discuss Cohen?

Solo: I went to Larry to do it originally, and he did a script which was pretty good. Then the executives changed at Warner Bros., and they wanted another writer, and then there was another executive, so it was one of those nightmarish studio relationships.

Timpone: Was it your idea to go more youth-oriented?

Solo: Yeah.

Timpone: Were you a fan of Stuart Gordon's horror films before you hired him to script the film with Dennis Paoli?

Solo: Yeah, Stuart did a very good script with Dennis. I thought that script was going to get shot. But it didn't because another new executive came in, and they gave him three or four scripts that they said needed looking over, and he looked at it and said, "Now I'm the executive of this project, and I loved your script." And then twenty-five drafts later...

Timpone: What made you replace Cohen and bring Gordon in?

Solo: It was the studio.

Timpone: Why do you think the film was cursed in its development and took so long to come together?

Solo: Well, we had an inept executive on it. He was completely inept, and every weekend he would see a movie and come back on Monday and say, "Look, we have to have a story meeting because I saw this movie over the weekend and we have to stick in this and we have to stick in that." It was just a nightmare.

Timpone: Is that part of the reason why the film is so unsure of itself, whether it's a sequel or a remake?

Solo: Well, ultimately I guess what happened was they got more secure the closer it got to the previous version.

Timpone: At any point, did United Artists make any kind of a fuss about the use of the pod scream or any other elements of the '78 version?

Solo: Actually, I don't know. After that movie I was out of there, I left L.A.

Timpone: It was such a bad experience that you just wanted to leave the business?

Solo: Yes, it was a terrible experience from start to finish, from the development stage through production and postproduction. For me, anyway.

Timpone: Was Abel Ferrara your replacement choice after Gordon left?

Solo: No, he was studio executive Lance Young's choice, and he sold him to the studio. He certainly wasn't my choice. I just thought he was the wrong jockey for the horse. While I like some of Abel's previous work, I just felt that he was inappropriate. He was great for gritty, realistic New York street movies, but had never done science fiction or had a flair for fantasy, and I just didn't think he was right for it. But ultimately, in a sense, he was given to me.

Timpone: Were any other directors considered who you preferred?

Solo: Yeah, there were other directors. Some directors didn't want to do it, they didn't want to make another remake or another version and so forth. But there was another very good director from Disney who wanted to do it, whose name I can't remember, and it came down to him or Abel, and the studio went for Abel.

Timpone: Was it Ferrara or Gordon's idea to toss the kid out of the helicopter at the end? That was pretty shocking.

Solo: I don't remember. I know that was a matter for some lengthy discussion with the studio. Should we or shouldn't we? This went on for quite a long time, and I was in favor of it, because I felt it was very shocking. And finally we shot it.

Timpone: Did you agree with Ferrara's decision to go back to the book and abandon some of the more visceral ideas that Gordon and Paoli had scripted—the pod people dissolving from the insecticide, for example?

Solo: That would have been more science fiction. And that's what Stuart does. That was a different approach, and I liked it because it was a very science fiction approach. After all, what are we selling? It isn't *War and Peace*, it isn't a love story. It's a science fiction movie, however you clothe it. Whatever the characters are like or the dialogue, it's a science fiction movie. You can't pretend it's not. Abel kept trying to make this not a science fiction movie. That was the problem; he didn't understand it. And when he was hired and went off with his pal, Nicky St. John, who's a very nice guy and not untalented, they came back with a draft where they took out all the pods! They took out everything that was science fiction! That was the plight—he never could get with what the material was, he could never get with it being science fiction. So he just kept trying to make it a New York street movie. When you've got a crew of eighty and you've got set designers and construction people, it's not the same as if you're making a movie with about twenty-five people in New York on 47th Street, and you want to shoot on 47th Street and traffic is too heavy so you say, "Let's run over to 46th Street." Which was the way he used to make movies. Well, you can't do that when you've got a crew of eighty-five and a regular schedule and sets are built and people have shooting schedules and so forth. You can't improvise like that. But that's the only kind of shooting he knows.

Timpone: So I take it this led to enormous friction between you and Ferrara?

Solo: Oh, terrible! Well, not personally. We had some words, but not personally. It was just that in effect finally I felt that I was in the hands of the wrong person, and the picture was going to be a disaster. I mean, I thought it was going to be a disaster, but it didn't turn out to be one. But it didn't turn out to be anything remotely like I hoped or expected it to be. He was, as I said, the wrong jockey for the horse.

Timpone: The film seems somewhat abbreviated at eighty-seven minutes. What wound up on the cutting room floor?

Solo: God knows. A lot of stuff. Dede Allen was under contract with Warner Bros. and was their in-house film editor, and she in effect oversaw the final cutting of the film. So by then I had really washed my hands of the picture. The postproduction was very prolonged and difficult.

Timpone: Is it true the film went over budget?

Solo: A lot.

Timpone: That must have caused trouble between you and the studio.

Solo: Well, my production manager, who was my line producer, quit about two days before we started shooting. The picture, because of Abel, was already a million dollars over and the camera hadn't turned! The production manager was an old-timer. I'd worked with him before and he knew his business, and he said, "I'm not going to be carried out of here feet first. I quit!"

Timpone: At any point, did you consider trying to replace Ferrara?

Solo: Candidly, yes. It was around that time. And Lance Young came down there and insisted that Abel stay on as director, and—well, what can I say?

Timpone: Why do you think *Body Snatchers* tested poorly when they finally got it out there in front of an audience?

Solo: I guess because it wasn't great! Most pictures test poorly because they're not terrific. So that's why it tested poorly. It ended up an OK movie. Not great and not terrible; it's an OK movie.

Timpone: At what point did you realize that Warner Bros. was going to dump the film?

Solo: After they saw it [laughs]! Just about after we had a preview. They thought so highly of the movie that they previewed it two miles away in Burbank. [Studio chiefs] Bob Daly and Terry Semel were basically horrified by the movie, and they sent the word out, "Guys, don't spend too much more money on this, just finish it and get it out of here." That's my guess.

Timpone: What do you think is the main problem with the film? Was it the fact that it abandoned those science fiction elements?

Solo: Well, it was a film that was neither here nor there, it really didn't have a point of view, it didn't have any engaging characters for the most part. Basically it had no prologue; you never really had time to get to know any of the people before it started. It all started happening too fast, and as a result most of the movie was one long chase.

Timpone: Didn't Ferrara keep the film alive by bringing it to Cannes?

Solo: Well, he tried, and they [Warner Bros.] were shocked that they chose it. And of course I was shocked, and nonetheless we all got a free ride to the Cannes festival, which was nice. And they all sat around, the Warners people, sort of surprised that the movie was even there. Abel was his usual self, he was late and unshaven. Abel was Abel.

Timpone: He is quite a character.

Solo: Yeah, Abel is a character unto himself. I don't dislike him as a person. I just wouldn't want anything to do with him professionally ever again.

Timpone: Four years later, you still sound pretty bitter about the whole thing.

Solo: Well, not bitter, just resigned to the fact that it was a project that started out with reasonably good credentials, and was gradually ground down by a studio executive who finally got fired. So that, coupled with the experience with Abel—I really took no moment of pleasure out of the experience. That's why I sound the way I do, not so much because the movie didn't turn out the way I wanted it to turn out, but because the experience was so unpleasant.

Timpone: In retrospect, would you do anything differently with the third film?

Solo: Well, I wouldn't hire Abel Ferrara in the first place; that's the first thing I wouldn't do. And then everything else would follow from that.

Timpone: If *Body Snatchers* had been the start of a franchise, which it was originally envisioned as, where else would you have taken the story besides Washington, D.C., which Gordon spoke about?

Solo: Yeah, exactly. They start coming into Washington, D.C. In the next one they get the president, they take over the government. Of course we all believe that everybody in Congress is a bunch of pods as it is, even now. So the idea is that they infiltrate the FBI, the CIA, and Congress and so on. And basically it's a kind of a coup. And what do you do with that, after that? I don't know the answer, but that's where it was going.

Timpone: Will you give the story another shot in a few years, or should it be laid to rest?

Solo: It's time to rest, it's time for a good long rest. Besides, other people rip it off all the time.

Timpone: Looking at the trio of films objectively, which do you think is the best version?

Solo: Well, I have to say mine.

Timpone: The '78?

Solo: Yeah, I just think so. I revere the old one and Don Siegel, but it wasn't nearly as sophisticated. And in addition to being scary, the movie that we did and Richter wrote was funny. It was sardonic, it was *very* hip for the time, it wasn't just your everyday science fiction movie. So I just think it was a much more sophisticated movie than either of the others, and that's why I like it the best. It's a smart movie.

Timpone: And the Hollywood system was a lot different in those days; you had much more control over the film.

Solo: Oh, yeah. Certainly with United Artists and Mike Medavoy, who was also a fan of Phil Kaufman's. He let us make the movie we wanted to make. As long as we brought it in on time, they really didn't interfere at all. There were only two or three executives; today there are twenty-seven thousand executives at every studio, and every one has an opinion.

Timpone: Why do you think audiences keep taking to Jack Finney's story?

Solo: Because we all think there's something under the bed. Ever since we were babies, little children, it was, "Mommy, don't close the door, leave the light on." There's something atavistic about it. We're terrified that somebody, something, is going to get us. The big bad wolf, the ghost, the bogeyman. That's just part of who we are as creatures at a very young age. So I think that's why audiences respond to it, it's something very basic to human nature.

Timpone: Before we go, is there anything else you would like to add about having worked on two *Body Snatchers* films?

Solo: Only to say that the experience I had with Phil Kaufman and Richter was terrific, and of all the movies I've made, working with Phil was the most pleasant experience of any of them, it was really a pleasure. One was pleasure, the other one was pain [laughs]!

THE MARK OF ABEL ON A CLASSIC: AN INTERVIEW WITH ABEL FERRARA

— — —

Gilbert Colon

Born in the Bronx on July 19, 1951, independent director Abel Ferrara has proven his considerable versatility at both television directing (episodes of *Miami Vice, Crime Story,* and *Subway Stories*) and feature filmmaking, starting with the low-budget thriller *The Driller Killer* (1979). It is only natural that he would eventually demonstrate his versatility with subject matter as well. Though widely known and regarded for his work in the crime genre with such infamous outings as *The King of New York* (1990) and *Bad Lieutenant* (1992), Ferrara burst onto the science fiction scene with his version of Jack Finney's classic, *The Body Snatchers.* Later, he went on to dabble in the horror genre with his black-and-white vampire opus, *The Addiction* (1995), before returning to the gritty urban morality plays that gained him notoriety with *The Blackout* (1997).

Ferrara immediately reveals a deep and obvious admiration for author Jack Finney, his book *The Body Snatchers,* director Don Siegel, and Siegel's film version *Invasion of the*

Body Snatchers. Indeed, a respect for science fiction as a whole comes through. Ferrara is currently continuing his work in the science fiction genre with a forthcoming adaptation of William Gibson's short story *New Rose Hotel.*

Gilbert Colon: First, I wanted to know how faithful you were determined to be to Jack Finney's novel, *The Body Snatchers.*

Abel Ferrara: Well, it was Jack Finney's novel that got me into doing it because I knew the concept intrigued me, and I found the theme interesting. The Martians become you and take you, but only your physicality—and then they are what they are, which in theory is a big improvement on man, from their point of view. They're *you* without the screaming and yelling. But then again, is that an improvement or what? But you see, in the book Finney really worked on the angle that this is at the beginning of nuclear testing, and he was into the idea that man was now jeopardizing not only the planet but actually the universe with what he's doin'. And that's one of the reasons that he wrote it; to say, "Hey dudes, you can fuck up your own place, but leave the rest of the universe to us Zen Buddhists."

Colon: So mainly you were striving to remain faithful to Finney's themes.

Ferrara: Yeah. His book's a wild work of imagination. Basically the Martians came to Earth to bring everybody the good news. Now the earthlings naturally react with their paranoia and, well, violence, and they basically say at one point, all right guys, bye-bye.

Colon: So you're almost sympathetic to the body snatchers?

Ferrara: Oh, very much so. Now who's gonna make a movie like that? Don Siegel was a little bit in that groove. In other words, he tried to make it as far away from the obvious good guy-bad guy business as he could and still not get murdered by the financiers. But they retooled the movie on him. The studio reshot the beginning and the ending. Those things were done a year later, even though I think Siegel was there. Siegel's version started with that beautiful shot of the train coming into the station, not the bullshit in the hospital and the FBI going after him and all the stuff told in flashback....

Colon: How different was Siegel's original vision?

Ferrara: Well, with the new opening, there's no tension anymore. Plus the music changed the whole thing.

Colon: By putting the story into a flashback frame, it becomes a happy ending.

Ferrara: Siegel's ending is when he sees them in the truck—great ending. They see a truck driving down the street—

Colon: And that's the real ending, or should've been the ending.

Ferrara: —and then we come back, and blow up

everybody. Not bad, except all you need is one pod. Then again, who knows if the seedlings have gone all over the world.

Colon: But your version kind of tricks you into believing it's a happy ending. Gabrielle Anwar and Billy Wirth blow the pods up en route, and you think for maybe just a fraction of a minute they won.

Ferrara: Humanity saves the day.

Colon: Maybe everything's okay. And then they land their helicopter and it's not quite that way.

Ferrara: They could've gotten them all.

Colon: After all that, they don't even know.

Ferrara: Nobody knows. I always wanted to get that ending. And let me say something about that end—that Phil Nielson, who's a great stunt coordinator who also works with director Oliver Stone, he makes it. He hates for me to say it, but he did second unit work on these scenes—I say that at great personal risk to myself. I would have never taken on a film about the military without Nielson seeing me through from the very start. There's nothing worse than a film dealing with the military taken from the point of view of a pacifist draft dodger like myself. See, although I respect those of my generation who fought and died in Vietnam, I equally respect those who protested the war—some at greater personal loss than me. There was a common enemy, which is again like *The Body Snatchers.* Either way you look at it, it's group thinking.

Colon: Did you see the Siegel version and Finney's book as paranoid polemics against communist subversion, or warnings against McCarthyist red-baiting? People are divided on whether the pod creatures are communists coming, invading, infiltrating, or the whole thing is a parable about the gathering forces of witchhunting....

Ferrara: Now what are we talking about? The story or the movie? Are you talking about the movie as Siegel made it, or the movie that was fucking jerry-rigged together?

Colon: So you see them as different?

Ferrara: Yeah, in other words, you slapdash that beginning and ending on—somebody walking across the street and you hear nuh nuh, nuh nuh, nuh nuh, *nuh nuh,* you're gonna say, "Oh, I'm scared." But if you take the music out, it's just someone walking across the street.... You dig what I'm sayin'? The film Siegel made's left-wing, the fuckin' movie they tried to turn it into was right-wing, so what do they got? A fuckin' middle-of-the-road movie! A movie is left-wing *and* right-wing. A movie's a work of art, man, it's not political propaganda. Siegel's an artist. I mean to me, Picasso's an artist. But if any film director can be an artist in this business, then Siegel fits the bill. He's an artist—that's his politics, man.

Colon: Which brings me to your personal politics. They sound—

Ferrara: Antipolitics.

Colon: Wow, that sums up something. I was going to say, from reading other interviews you sound a bit like Vincent Gallo's communist character in *The Funeral.* And I wondered if you put any of that into *Body Snatchers?*

Ferrara: Most of communist politics is actually a fascistic mindset—to control and achieve power rather than uplift. I'm a limousine liberal.

Colon: Did that bent affect your decision to set the story on a military base?

Ferrara: I didn't set it on a military base.

Colon: That was in the original draft?

Ferrara: I don't know which draft it was, but that was the Solo people. They didn't want me to change it and I didn't feel like arguing it, 'cause it's definitely—

Colon: As good a place as any?

Ferrara: No, it's not as good as any. But it's 180 degrees from the fuckin' point of the story. The point of the story is you are not who you appear to be. How do I know if you're not who you are if I don't know you? But if I know you from when we were kids I can say, jeez, you're not acting like you. In the book a great scene is him lookin' at the librarian who gave him his first copy of *Huckleberry Finn* and saying, "I know who you are." She says, "Do you?" It's a great line. The idea is truly beautiful. It's like, it's ambiguity. It's complexity. I wanted to do that film because the complexity of the source material transcends a particular zeitgeist of mid-fifties Americana. Like a lot of good science fiction, it's metaphor. But to try to simplify it, to say this is about, y'know, fuckin' communism or nuclear testing or whatever, it's too simplistic. You trivialize it. The book—it's beautiful. It's a metaphor like an image in a million mirrors—y'know what I mean? It's infinite.

Colon: Many of your films, like *Body Snatchers,* have very sympathetic portrayals of female characters—do you have feminist leanings?

Ferrara: We dig the bitches.

Colon: Were you approached by the studio, or did you seek the project out?

Ferrara: They came to us. Who would come up with this thing? It's an odd film for Warner Bros. to make, right? But you know, the way I looked at it was—not to compare ourselves to the Rolling Stones, we're not—it was like that band covering a Chuck Berry song, y'know? We're connecting to somebody else's shit.

Colon: Do you know how they chose you specifically?

Ferrara: No, I mean obviously it was Stuart Gordon and Larry Cohen. They were sniffing for that genre of director. I think they talked to a lot of guys like me, and I was the one who gave them the right bullshit. They definitely wanted bad guys and action, which I gave them. Warners Bros. basically wrote their own version. They had your typical mental midget script. I shouldn't say Warner Bros., and I'm not blamin' any of the screenwriters. I mean, on my version of the script we have five names, which I love, and somebody put a fake name on it, I think.

Colon: What was the fake name?

Ferrara: I don't know, but why put a bum name on it? Why not just not put one on?

Colon: I know it wasn't your longtime collaborator Nicholas St. John, obviously. Larry Cohen and Stuart Gordon—they're established names. And Dennis Paoli's scripted projects for Gordon, so it's not him. That leaves Raymond Cistheri, whose last screen credit was the film *Melinda* back in 1972.

Ferrara: Who knows. The bottom line is, I never met any of those guys and wouldn't know 'em if I fell over 'em. I think one of 'em came around at the end when we had one of the advance screenings and was sitting there with one of the fuckin' Warner Bros. executives and he's like, y'know, smarter than a fucking kitty cat and put his two cents in. He's there at the fucking screening at that point and he's fighting for some dumb thing he wrote.

Colon: By now it's too late.

Ferrara: It's *not* too late. If you got a problem with the film, talk to me in private. Don't talk about it in front of the executives. But he was one of these guys running up to the executives because he knew he might— y'know what I'm sayin'? Just an asshole. I wanted to say to him, That's my film, don't be fucking things up.

Colon: Was there a whole lot of resemblance to the first draft?

Ferrara: Are you kiddin' me? They were into the idea that the Martians were vegetables, y'know what I mean? But they were pods! I never understood where the vegetable routine came from.

Colon: I remember reading that they wanted to make even their insides vegetable matter.

Ferrara: Yeah, I mean this is ludicrous, a total misunderstanding.... But I guess they didn't give a shit. The original idea is that they totally duplicated whatever you were—they weren't vegetables on the inside, they were you. But these guys had somebody cutting them open with a letter opener and, y'know, stupid shit exploding out of them. I mean, *do you know how stupid that is?*

Colon: Did the studio like that?

Ferrara: I guess so. I mean, the studio, they were weird. There was the producer Robert H. Solo and there was a hotshot young [production] executive named Lance Young and he was the executive regime's model. They were muscling him out, so it was a period of transition. Young was a closet writer-director anyway—he went on to write and direct his own movie, *Bliss* (1997).

Colon: Was there any interference on *Body Snatchers* by studio heads?

Ferrara: They were there. Dede Allen was one of their editors. At least the person they had tampering with the film was solid. I mean, Dede's a two-time Oscar-nominated editor. She cut *Bonnie and Clyde* (1967), *Dog Day Afternoon* (1975), and *Reds* (1981). But nobody, *nobody* ever wants someone screwing around with his film. But I knew when I got involved that I didn't have final cut. I knew that. I didn't have the juice at the time to demand it, and I still took the film, so I'm not gonna be fuckin' vicious about it. I knew what I was getting. It wasn't as bad as it could have been, and then at the same time somebody changes one fucking shot and it's hard. But I've had it worse having final cut, believe it or not. In other words, when people are in your face twenty-four hours a day, seven days a week—which the studio is when you're making that type of film—I don't care whether you have final cut or not, if somebody's sayin': "That shot's no good, that shot's no good, that shot's no good, that shot's no good, that shot's no good"—y'know what I mean? You could have final cut and after a while you're gonna be thinking, jeez, maybe that shot's no good.

Colon: You're going to doubt, right?

Ferrara: It's not just that, it's all kinds of things. Because when we do a film where we have total control, where I write the checks, it's different. But if somebody else has control—in a way I had more freedom not having final cut at Warners. It's ironic. They are *very* aware of their reputation as a studio. They were conscious of that. You see, they don't want it getting out that Warners fucks over directors. They have to be very careful, or word will spread and the directors they want they're not going to be able to get. If they want Oliver Stone they won't be able to get him if he thinks they're going to ruin his film. And another plus for the studio is if a film's a failure, you as the director carry the blame, not them. They don't want some director pointing a finger at them and saying, "The studio made me do that." Take for instance, even though they didn't want Gabrielle Anwar for *Body Snatchers*, they didn't stop me from casting her either. This way if the film's a bust, they can blame me.

Colon: Did you lose anything from *Body Snatchers* that you still regret?

Ferrara: That's hard to say. I dig the film. I'll stand

behind the film as it is. There's one cut that I fuckin' can't stand, but—

Colon: Which one was that? Do you want to say?

Ferrara: I don't remember. But I'll tell you one thing, that film was in competition at Cannes, despite what Warners eventually did with it.

Colon: Apart from the body snatcher's piercing wail—

Ferrara: That was Solo. It came from the second film, which he also produced.

Colon: —was there any attempt to apply continuity or compatibility with the other two films?

Ferrara: We stole everything that wasn't nailed down.

Colon: Would you call Body Snatchers a remake, a sequel, or something else?

Ferrara: It was another interpretation of someone's novella, the third interpretation.

Colon: I know you like the first film, except for the tampering.... How about the Philip Kaufman remake—did you enjoy his interpretation?

Ferrara: It took me a long time to appreciate the second one.

Colon: How long?

Ferrara: It took me *a longer* time to appreciate the second, y'know what I'm saying? Then I saw where they were comin' from. I thought, maybe if I see it enough I'll dig it. The thing is, Siegel's is a tough film to top, y'know what I mean? And again, I just didn't quite get Kaufman's at first. I saw both of them a lot of times. The second—it took me a while to get into the groove of it. So I feel I just can't talk about that one like I can the first one. I thought I understood the first one better, that's all. I'm not sayin' one is better than the other.

Colon: Was the chance to work with state-of-the-art special effects on a science fiction film a lure for you?

Ferrara: We used Tom Burman, the same guy they used for the second film. I didn't want any of that morphing.

Colon: You could have, but you chose not to?

Ferrara: At $18 million, we didn't have the budget to compete with $70-80 million effects films, so we didn't try. We didn't have the budget of *Twister,* so we kept things simple—reverse motion, and just Burman's work. The guy, he's like the rest of us, know what I mean? He fucks up as much as he doesn't, but he can knock you out when he hits it. Besides, I don't go for postproduction effects. I'm a what-you-see-is-what-you-get kind of guy anyway. I don't want to wait two years later to see what's up on screen.

Colon: Did you tell Burman to do anything different than he did on the second film?

Ferrara: What we did different was work with Bojan Bazelli. So, y'know, we had a great cine-

matographer. I respect him. That movie was
pure CinemaScope, not thirtyfive millimeter
blown up. How often do you see that?

Colon: Stuart Gordon's script was supposedly signif-
icantly more graphic in nature.

Ferrara: How can a draft be graphic? It's words on
paper. His was ridiculous. Somebody gets cut
and all of a sudden, fuckin' spinach pops out.
How can that be scary? It's ludicrous.

Colon: I guess that's considered graphic.

Ferrara: Graphic? Spinach poppin' out of people.
How the fuck graphic is that? Who are
they?! Popeye?! Get the fuck out of here! I
mean, the whole thing with these types of
films is to make them play as if they can
happen. I mean, whatever anybody says, the
fuckin' movie I made, *that* could happen. It's
a very scary movie, if I do say so myself. I
don't mind saying that because I'm not the
only one who made it, y'know what I'm
sayin'? I didn't write it, I didn't shoot it, I
didn't do the effects and I didn't act in it.
What I'm tryin' to say, when I watch that
film, it's not cinemafantastique, y'know
what I mean? It's like, oh man, why not? I
mean, if you have any imagination for other-
worldly events, why is that not a possibility?

Colon: Maybe because it was restrained, it seemed
very plausible for the kind of scenario it
was....

Ferrara: Sure is, man. I mean, the first one was like

the fuckin' *Bicycle Thief,* y'dig what I'm sayin'? The black-and-white, the way they acted and all that stuff. If it wasn't for the ill-suited music—that wasn't Siegel's thing, man. That was never there. Forget it, man. I mean, it's too fuckin' bad there's not a version of it somebody could put together

Colon: A director's cut?

Ferrara: Yeah, maybe I'll do it. That'd be a presumptuous thing to do. The director's cut of Don Siegel's movie, by Abel Ferrara. Why not? I should. We have all the reasons to. Take the front and back off, and dump all that inappropriate music.

Colon: *Body Snatchers*—they envisioned it as a franchise.

Ferrara: But we ended it [both laugh]! We put a stop to that!

Colon: Would you ever direct another one if you were asked, and what direction would you go?

Ferrara: I'd try to do the whole story.

Colon: *Body Snatchers* didn't screen well, like a lot of genre films don't.

Ferrara: Right.

Colon: But tell me, do you ever go by test screenings?

Ferrara: I'll try and get something from it, but not the way they would. Anytime you got a film in front of the audience, you should learn something.

Colon: Next up for you is *New Rose Hotel,* which you're in production for. Are you a fan of William Gibson?

Ferrara: I am now.

Colon: What did you feel about *Johnny Mnemonic?*

Ferrara: I didn't see it.

Colon: Are there any future plans to return to your other political science fiction project, *Birds of Prey?*

Ferrara: I don't want to talk about *Birds of Prey.* It's a film I've wanted to make for a long time. Twenty years and the idea's still viable and original.

Colon: Is that your script?

Ferrara: It's Nicky's [St. John.]

Colon: Mainly you work in the crime genre. Is science fiction a favorite genre of yours?

Ferrara: I dug a lot of it when I was a kid. It's like nostalgia. I remember seeing *The Blob* with my father and him falling asleep in the theater, and me not waking him up till I saw it twice. I got my ass kicked for that one.

THE UNSEEN BODY SNATCHERS

— — —

Anthony Timpone

As just about any filmmaker working in the movies today can tell you, it's a miracle that any film gets made under the labyrinthine, bureaucratic Hollywood system. Endless corporate meetings, the fitful development process, mutating screenplays, etc., are enough to make one reconsider that job offer from McDonald's.

Body Snatchers, producer Robert H. Solo's second redux of the Jack Finney novel, was no exception. The screenplay went through at least twenty drafts and six scripters before Warner Bros. greenlit the film for production in the fall of 1991. One of the credited screenwriters, cult director Stuart Gordon (best known for the shock sleepers *Re-Animator, From Beyond, Dolls* and *The Pit and the Pendulum),* was also hired to direct the film. But frustrated by the development quagmire, Gordon jumped ship to pilot 1993's futuristic actioner *Fortress* instead.

The Chicago-born Gordon and his longtime writing partner Dennis Paoli took *Body Snatchers* through four drafts before Gordon handed the reins over to controversial director Abel Ferrara *(Bad Lieutenant),* who then brought in his writing buddy, Nicholas St. John, to take a few more whacks at the script. (The final film is credited to Gordon and Paoli and St. John, from a story by Larry Cohen and Raymond Cistheri.) After all the start-up delays, *Body Snatchers* suffered further indignities when dissatisfied distributor Warner Bros. shelved the sequel/remake for nearly two years, only giving the decently reviewed film a marginal theatrical release in the spring of 1994.

In the following interview, Gordon discusses *Body Snatchers's* troubled birth and delivery, and reveals some surprising differences between his and Paoli's initial take on the project and what ultimately emerged.

<table>
<tr><td>Anthony
Timpone:</td><td>What guidelines did Robert Solo give you when he hired you to direct and cowrite *Body Snatchers?*</td></tr>
<tr><td>Stuart
Gordon:</td><td>He asked me to come in so we could pitch an idea. He'd sent me the script they had been working on, which Larry Cohen had written. What they were trying to do was to make it a sequel to the seventies movie. The main idea was to make it more youth-oriented and have the characters be younger. Larry's version is all about these teenagers, kids, people in their early twenties. The army base was not in it until the last act of the story. Originally it was my idea to make it about a family, but I felt that we didn't care enough about the kids [in Cohen's version]. It was more like a *Halloween* kind of thing going on, where the kids are getting bumped off one by one. I felt that it would be more upsetting with a family being taken over one at a time, the idea being that we</td></tr>
</table>

wouldn't be sure who the protagonist was for a little while, and it would turn out to be the teenage daughter.

In the story setup, the characters are based on my family, right down to their names. My wife's name is Carolyn, and Marti, the daughter, is based on my daughter Suzanna. The reason we called her Marti was because when I brought Dennis Paoli in to write it with me, we were both envisioning Martha Plimpton in the role, so we named the character after her. As it turned out, the producers thought that she was too old by the time the movie finally would be cast, so we got Gabrielle Anwar, who I thought was great.

What we were trying to do was bring back the movie as a franchise, which Warner Bros. wanted. With *Body Snatchers,* Bob Solo had brought up the idea of making several movies, and mine could be part one. The ending of our movie had the trucks being sent out with the pods to all the various military bases, but they're also being sent to Washington, D.C. The last shot in our script was of the trucks driving down Pennsylvania Boulevard. And one of the things Bob Solo and I talked about was the next movie involving the president of the United States, the idea of the government being taken over by pods. That was where the next *Body Snatchers* movie was going, almost like Romero's *Living Dead* movies, that the whole world was going to be eventually taken over by pod people.

Timpone: How much of Cohen's original script wound up in the final film?

Gordon: Not much, really. The idea of the army base was the main idea that survived, which is really the last third of the story in Larry's version. Most of the story took place in this town. Our first draft actually took place in the town. In the second draft, Bob Solo and the studio suggested the idea that the whole thing should take place at the army base.

Originally, in our version, we had the town being taken over by fundamentalists. There was this whole church thing going on, the born-again thing. When they were taken over by body snatchers, they were born again in a way. But we sided to the idea that maybe the army base was something we hadn't seen before. While we were working on it, the studio realized that it had been so long since the seventies movie that the idea of this being a sequel to that one didn't make any sense. So instead, they decided that maybe it should be thought of as a whole new version of *Invasion of the Body Snatchers.*

Timpone: So at first it was pitched as a sequel, and then it was decided to make it more of a remake. The completed film is stuck somewhere in between.

Gordon: Yeah, it was. It was funny, because we borrowed things from both the first two movies. Some of the ideas, like the pod scream from

the second film, we incorporated into ours.
We also had things that got cut out of the
film. I was originally supposed to direct the
film, but then we were prepping the picture
for so long, doing rewrites, in development
hell and so forth, and I was offered *Fortress*.
So I went off to do that instead. They got
Abel Ferrara to come in, and he dropped a
few of the things that we had developed.

When we were brought on, we were asked
to try to make the thing scarier and more
explicit than the earlier films. And one of
the ideas that we came up with was the
thought that the body snatchers, the pod
people, look like human beings on the outside, but inside they're nothing like human
beings. They are sort of mimicking the look
of a human being, which was a departure
from the original story. The original story
idea is that they take over humans molecule
by molecule in their duplication. We got
into this idea that inside they're like a plant
and that their organs work unlike human
organs and that, like a plant, their ability to
think is cellular, rather than them having a
brain and a nervous system and so forth.
And so if you were to chop the head off
these pod people, for example, they could
still function. So we did a lot of bits like that.
There's one sequence in [our script] where
the pod people are chasing after them and
they go into a garage, and the heroes begin
using tools in the garage to try to defend

themselves. Things like garden shears and spades, chopping off their fingers, which doesn't seem to have any effect on them. Shooting them has no effect either, and finally Marti ends up grabbing a sprayer that's got some weed killer in it and sprays them with it. They start to dissolve with the weed killer, which led to the finale where they drop a defoliant, Agent Orange, on the plant people to kill them. That was a concept that we played with, and we even had Berni Wrightson do some illustrations to show how this would work, which looked pretty incredible, drawings of them dissolving and their insides being all over, looking like an eggplant or something.

Timpone: Why do you think that material was cut from subsequent drafts of the film?

Gordon: It happened when Abel came on. He wanted to stick more closely to the original concept and book, which was that they were completely duplicate human beings. They dispensed with it, although there were still elements of it at the end of the movie. They still drop and spray the defoliant on them, and they do dissolve, which is kind of unexplained.

Timpone: Were there any other graphic moments in your script that never made it into the film?

Gordon: Well, there was a cut sequence that I liked a lot that was actually from Larry Cohen's draft that we put into the beginning of our script. This guy is watching these bulldozers pushing thousands of what's left of the bodies into a big pit, and then covering the pit up in this massive burial scene. They see him and he's running, and these big earth movers are chasing after him, trying to push him into the hole as well. And [in the completed film] that soldier is the one who's in the gas station who grabs Marti; he's hysterical, freaking out. We had envisioned it being almost like a pretitle sequence. It could have been a very effective scene.

Timpone: Reportedly, United Artists, the distributor of the 1978 film, was upset that Warner Bros. had appropriated elements from their film for an unauthorized "sequel," the pod people scream being an example. Do you know anything about that?

Gordon: No. We were encouraged to use the scream. The garbage truck idea was in some of the drafts that we did, the idea of the aliens taking over the bodies and throwing them in the garbage truck, which is in the second film. So we were told by Bob Solo that anything he had developed in his version we could use in this one, that it was a sequel. Dennis Paoli used to kid around that we were making a sequel to a remake [laughs].

Timpone: At some point, Stephen King was approached to do a rewrite. Did you have discussions with him?

Gordon: Actually, I never had any discussions, but it

was our idea. What happened was typical studio fashion. We had done about three or four drafts of the script. They said, "We'd like to bring in a new writer to rewrite it." So they asked us who we would suggest. We wanted to shoot high and we said Stephen King, so they sent him the script and got a wonderful letter back from him which I've saved, which said, "I really was interested in doing this, but I read the script and there's an old adage, 'If it ain't broke, don't fix it.' This script is great and you should just shoot it. You don't need me." But the studio didn't agree with him, apparently, so they brought in a couple more writers to do drafts.

Timpone: Next at bat was writer Nevin Schreiner. Did you collaborate with him directly?

Gordon: Yeah, I did.

Timpone: He replaced Dennis at that point?

Gordon: Yeah, he did. His stuff didn't change all that much.

Timpone: Was Schreiner someone that Solo brought in or was it Warner Bros.?

Gordon: No, actually what happened was weird. At this point, I was still the director of the film, so I was interviewing other writers. I interviewed several people, and thought that he had the best take on where to go from there.

Timpone: What impressed you about his take?

Gordon: He had a good feeling about the characters.

What we wanted to do was try to make the characters as real as we could, and he had a good concept. I liked his dialogue and I liked the fact that he could flesh them out a little bit more. And he was not into doing a total overhaul. The thing that I was afraid of was, when you bring in new writers, they always want to make it their own. They end up throwing out everything that you've done, and it starts over again. I did not want to do that. I liked the way we had developed it, we'd done fresh work on it and he fine-tuned what we did without any major over-haul. When Abel Ferrara replaced me as director, he brought in Nicholas St. John. There were several changes that they did, the main one being the changing of the pod people's physiology. But he also changed the character of the pilot.

Timpone: The Billy Wirth character?

Gordon: Yeah. In our version—which I liked better, actually—he was a guy who pretended to be a pilot in order to pick up girls, and it turns out that he is actually in the helicopter ground crew. And in the climactic sequence, when he's got to make the escape and he gets into the helicopter, he doesn't know how to fly one! He's able to escape because he has been working around them and knows what the various things do, but he's never actually flown one before. So it was a much scarier thing. You've got this guy try-ing to take off in a helicopter who doesn't know how to fly. And you end up with the question of whether he's gonna be able to land it, if he's going to land it. But they decided at some point, I don't know whose decision it was, to make him more of a hero, a big hero from Kuwait, and references to him being an ace helicopter pilot.

Timpone: Coming from the independent scene, what was it like working for a major studio on *Body Snatchers?*

Gordon: Well, there were a lot of committee discussions, and that was the thing that got to be very frustrating, because different people have different thoughts. The thing about studios sometimes is that whatever movie happens to be hot that particular week, they want you to make your movie like that. I remember at one point having a discussion with an executive who had just seen *Terminator 2*. There's that whole sequence where Linda Hamilton is shooting from the back of a truck, and he thought we should have a scene like that in our movie. But looking back at the whole thing, the people were all very supportive of the project. There was a sense that everybody really wanted to make it happen and make it good. A lot of times on a studio film, you get involved with people with different agendas, and on *Body Snatchers* everyone was for it. But studios are slow-moving entities. That was the thing that just got to me. If this had been a low-budget movie, we would have had it shot and out in theaters in a year, and with the studio it just ended up taking at least two and a half years. The process is mind-boggling.

Timpone: Were you a fan of the '56 and '78 films?

Gordon: Yeah, yeah. As a matter of fact, the Don Siegel version is still the best. The energy in that movie is incredible. I like the second one, although I don't think it holds up as well. We watched both movies again while we were working on ours, and the one in the fifties seemed much fresher, much more involving. But [director] Phil Kaufman was very much a child of the seventies, so it stays there.

It's funny, when I was working on *Body Snatchers* I ran into Kevin McCarthy. When I told him I was working on the third *Body Snatchers,* he said, "I have to be in it," because he had been in both of the first two films. In our version, the doctor was kind of an older man, and we thought that he'd be great to play the doctor.

Timpone: Which character is that in Ferrara's film? Major Collins?

Gordon: Yeah, the character that Forest Whitaker plays.

Timpone: That would have been a totally different character then.

Gordon: Yeah, but I liked what Forest Whitaker did a lot; he was great in the movie. Abel did a terrific job with it, and the performances he got were sensational. And I actually would go so far and say it is Abel's best movie.

Timpone: What do you think were some of the strengths of the first two adaptations?

Gordon: Well there's something kind of primal and nightmarish about the first film, and the energy is incredible. It really builds to a very powerful conclusion, and it's one of those few movies that has such a bleak ending; it's so downbeat and terrifying. The version in the seventies did much more with the special effects; they had gone further to show how the bodysnatching process was accomplished. That was one of the greatest strengths of the '78 film, the wispy things connecting the pod to the person, showing you how it happens. In the first version you didn't see any of that. All you saw of what the person became was when they find this half-formed pod person in the basement. And in the second version they show you the whole process, and how it's accomplished. At the time EST was very big, and that pop psychology thing was going on. The first movie was really about the Cold War and the fear of communists being among us, some of our friends being not really who they say they are and so forth. The second movie was much more in terms of people being taken over by cults like the Moonies. But the thing I got into that was in both movies was the issue of conformity.

That you are made to be like everybody else. That's what the pod people are. One of the things that you wrestle with in this is, "What is so terrible about being taken and being made into a pod person? You're still you." But what's missing is those things about you that make you an individual. There's a collective mind that connects them all. What we got into is that, in a sense, the reason that the teenager works as the heroine in the third one is because she's rebellious. What's considered to be her bad trait saves her. Which was what we were going for—the fact that she is the rebel, that she's a nonconformist, she's not really part of her family, that she's not going along with the program, is what makes her able to survive.

Timpone: What were the main elements that you wanted to bring to your take from the previous sources, Finney's book and the films?

Gordon: Well, the whole thing is a big paranoid fantasy, and I love how each begins in a very subtle, insidious way. I love the way it starts out with people coming into the doctor saying, "Oh, my uncle isn't my uncle. My father doesn't seem like my father; there's something wrong." It kind of underlined the delusional paranoia, which is what the doctor thinks is going on at first. There's some sort of a mass hysteria growing in town. When the first movie came out, it tied in with the McCarthy hearings during the Cold War—is my neighbor a communist? People are turning in their family members and so forth. That is the core of what all the *Body Snatchers* are about. It's not a monster movie, in that these guys aren't turning into vampires, or sucking your blood or anything. They go about their business as usual. But they're not really who they are. They're not human. What I really like about it is that it is a very subtle fear.

Timpone: Did you go back to Finney's book when you began this?

Gordon: Oh yes, absolutely. We read the book and as a matter of fact, the title of the third movie is the title of the book, *Body Snatchers.* We originally called our script *Body Snatchers: The Harvest.*

Timpone: Of the three films, which do you think captures Finney's themes the best?

Gordon: I've got to say the first movie. The first film is really Finney's book. It's remarkably close. Although Finney's book actually has a happy ending. The pods start lifting off and floating away; they leave the Earth at the end of the book. When the hero realizes what's going on and figures out how to destroy them, the pods retreat, where in Siegel's movie he gave it a much darker ending. The second one went even further with the ending than Siegel originally intended.

Timpone: You had come up with different endings when you were drafting your script, right?

Gordon: We did, yeah. One of the things the studio did, which I think was done against Abel's wishes too, was that they added this whole voice-over thing in the movie. Which I didn't want—I hate those things, first of all. We wanted the audience not to know who the hero of the movie was initially. They think the hero is going to be the dad, the Terry Kinney part.

Timpone: With the voice-over, you know from the start that the heroine will somehow survive.

Gordon: Right, that's what bothered me the most about it, because it lets you know she's gonna make it. So the voice-over takes away a lot of the tension in the movie. That was one of the notes we got; they wanted it to be clear that this was Marti's movie. I like it better when you don't know. We used *Alien* as a model, where you think the hero of the movie is Tom Skerritt, and then he gets wiped out halfway through. At the end, it's Sigourney Weaver who emerges as the hero of the film. So we were going with similar thinking. But when they started testing the film, it wasn't testing well, so they ended up, out of desperation, using the voice-over.

Timpone: Did you consider having a downbeat ending?

Gordon: Well, we wanted to actually leave it open, and in a way the movie's ending is close to what we had, though we went even further. In some of our endings, when they landed it turned out that where they went ended up being taken over by pod people. So they were tossed out of the frying pan into the fire. But I think we got to an ambiguous ending, where we're not sure who these people are and where they flew to at the end.

Timpone: When Ferrara came on board with Nicholas St. John, he said he wanted to "fix" problems in the third act of your script. How would you respond to that?

Gordon: Well, I guess what he meant was that he did not want to go the way we were going, which was the whole idea of this sort of different internal working system for the pod people.

Timpone: At any point, did Solo ask you to write another sequel or promise you another film as a consolation prize, especially after Ferrara replaced you?

Gordon: No, we never really got into anything like that, but if the thing had succeeded, there would have been another movie. I have remained friends with Bob Solo; he's a terrific guy. And he had a real hard time getting the movie out, because it did not test well. Warner Bros. got scared of it and was going to dump it. They would not even risk [a theatrical release]. It was Abel who got it shown at the Cannes Film Festival, just on his own, which forced Warner Bros. to actually release the movie.

Timpone: How much of yours and Paoli's script was retained in the completed film after St. John took over?

Gordon: It's funny. Almost beat for beat it's there, with the exceptions of the things we talked about, in terms of changing the character of Billy Wirth. But all the events that are happening are basically scene for scene the same as our script. Again, in typical screenwriter fashion, the dialogue was all changed; a lot of it is almost like paraphrasing what we had done. In the beginning of Abel's movie, he has them singing a song about going to eat worms. In our version we had them playing a game called "Who am I," which is this kid's game where you have to give clues about somebody, and then you have to guess who it is. The scene [in the final film] is basically the same scene, with them driving in the car and playing a game and the character of Marti excluding herself from it all, listening to her Walkman while all this is going on. So I think the whole movie is like that. If you were to put the two scripts side by side, the structure would pretty much be the same.

Timpone: Is there anything that St. John and Ferrara added that you especially liked?

Gordon: The bit with the truth game and the fingers was not in our script, which I thought was a real nice bit, I liked that. But I think our idea of having the relationship with the pilot who's not a pilot was more interesting than him being this big jock war hero character. But they wanted him to be cooler. I thought he was more funny if he was more vulnerable. Some of the things that were added improved it and some of the things didn't.

Timpone: At least six writers worked on *Body Snatchers;* did it ever wind up going to Writer's Guild arbitration?

Gordon: Oh yeah, it did. In this kind of situation they ended up giving everybody a piece of it, including W. D. Richter, who wrote the version in the seventies, but who had nothing to do with ours. But the Writer's Guild's arbitration manual says that in order to be credited, your work has to reflect 60 percent of the script. Ours had more in common with Finney's book than with the seventies remake.

Timpone: Why do you think Warner Bros. dumped the film?

Gordon: When you look at Warner's history, they have not done very many horror films, and the ones they have done have been these big-studio kind of things. They're not really scary. The studio is dependent upon marketing, test scores, and so forth, and when they got the test score on *Body Snatchers,* at that point they said, "Let's forget this." And what they forgot is that horror films notoriously test low. A lot of times when you get a test audience in there, you're not getting people who would go out and buy a ticket to this thing. You're getting people who don't like horror films or science fiction, so the test scores reflect that. Plus *Body Snatchers* was very disturbing. It's not your typical Hollywood finale where everything looks real great at the end. And that certainly was disturbing to people and made it test badly. At that point, Warners felt it would not be a big crowd-pleaser and wanted to move on. They were going to just release it direct to video. Then Abel, bless his heart, got it official entry at the Cannes Festival, where it got really good reviews and a French theatrical release. Warner Bros. felt silly and decided to release it, but by that point they just gave it a tokenistic release, almost as an art film. They gave it a platform release, put it out in a few theaters in the big cities. It did pretty well, but they never really gave it the push that it needed. Besides being Abel's best work, it's also Gabrielle Anwar's best movie. And if Warner Bros. had gotten behind the film, they could have made her into a major star.

Timpone: Do you think the film would have been more successful commercially if you had directed it and gone with your more graphic horror approach?

Gordon: I would honestly say no. Abel did a really good job with it; the movie was scary. Having that stuff maybe would have added more gross-out potential, but I don't think it would have been the difference between making or breaking the film. It really had to do with the studio not marketing it. That's really what killed the movie.

Timpone: Overall, would you say you're proud of your association with the film?

Gordon: Yeah, I'm very proud and I'm even prouder of being part of the *Body Snatcher* legacy. Going back to the book and the fifties movie, it's a true classic. To have the opportunity to be part of that is a great thing, and so I'm very happy that I was involved and very happy with the movie that resulted.

Timpone: Do you think these themes will be just as resonant in the twenty-first century as they are today?

Gordon: Oh yeah, absolutely, and I think that it's still possible that, knowing Bob Solo, there will be another Body Snatchers movie. Maybe it will be the one where the pod people take over Washington.

Dana Wynter and Kevin McCarthy

WILL THE REAL FINALE PLEASE TAKE A BOW?

— — —

Tom Piccirilli

"Many had lost, but some of us who had not been caught and trapped without a chance had fought implacably, and a fragment of a wartime speech moved through my mind: *we shall fight them in the field, and in the streets, we shall fight in the hills; we shall never surrender.* True then for one people, it was true for the whole human race, and now I thought that nothing in the whole vast universe could ever defeat us."

So states the heroic Dr. Miles Bennell at the conclusion of Jack Finney's novel *The Body Snatchers* (Award Books, 1965), after the pods themselves desert the earth in a mass exodus to float once again against the nighttime sky, leaving a "fierce and inhospitable planet." It is quite possibly one of the most overconfident, self-assured, and expectant declarations ever made in so horrifying a novel of anxiety and personal dread. After Bennell finally finds his way to the acres of pod-strewn fields, where they lie "evil and motionless" at his feet, he and his love Becky manage to spill drums of gasoline and set the fields afire.

At first there is no reaction from the overtaken friends and citizens of Mill Valley, who quickly surround the hunted pair and simply stare without any curiosity, anger, or emotion at all. Within moments, though, Miles and Becky

watch as the pods lift off for unknown worlds, the concept
being that any fight that went on for a lengthy duration
would be more than enough to drive away these incredibly
adaptive extraterrestrial survivors from our planet. Such a
sudden twist of fortuitous developments doesn't quite hold
together for those of us encompassed by the finely
wrought atmosphere of pure maddening fear created
beforehand.

The disturbing theme of the novel was open to diverse
interpretations, including issues of paranoia toward communism or the sweeping McCarthyism of the fifties, and
yet despite the broiling political pit the world was facing in
that era, of all versions of *The Body Snatchers* this is clearly
the most optimistic conclusion where the fate of the
human race is concerned. Even the "revised and updated"
edition of the novel in 1978—written to coincide with the
release of Philip Kaufman's movie version—the tale
remains one of heartening promise and hopefulness in the
midst of a mind-numbing whirlwind of alarm.

Don Siegel's 1956 classic adaptation, though, manages to
deepen the horror we're left to endure afterward, if only by
one additional frightening element. Kevin McCarthy, as
Miles Bennell, squeezes every possible drop of shock and
apprehension from his outstanding performance, his crisis
and distress escalating moment to moment. The viewer is
treated to the wraparound prologue/epilogue where we
find the distraught and seemingly psychotic Miles relating
his nightmarish tale to doctors in the emergency room.
Although the doctors comment that he is "mad as a March
hare," Miles is soon vindicated. His story is verified when a
Greyhound bus and a truck coming out of Santa Mira
(replacing Mill Valley) collide, and there's mention that
the truck driver has to be dug out from under "great big
seed pods." Soon law enforcement and government agen-

cies promise to take control of the invading aliens by blocking highways.

The single most startling moment of the film might very well be where Becky is "snatched" in a scene of raw terror, veering from the original happy ending of the novel. After escaping into a mine, and barely evading the swarming pod folk, Miles lifts and carries his fatigued love through the tunnel, leaving her for a minute to check if the coast is clear. In a scene that has gone down in the history of horror filmdom as one of the most gripping ever, he kisses Becky and slowly draws back in revulsion from her cold, unresponsive lips, realizing that she's fallen asleep and been overtaken. Despite the fact that the situation is somewhat loosely threaded (Becky apparently falls asleep and is somehow "possessed" by the pod swarm mind, rather than actually being grown from a pod) there is a fundamentally evocative and genuinely disturbing realization that causes real shudders in the viewer.

By 1978, however, Philip Kaufman had decided to follow variations of themes from its predecessor, creating not so much a remake of the original film as an elaboration of issue and milieu. Set in San Francisco now, Donald Sutherland, starring as "Matthew" Bennell, is a public health inspector ably assisted by Brooke Adams as Elizabeth. When the city becomes covered in what appear to be spiderwebs, Adams is the first to notice strange behavior in people, beginning with her boyfriend, who becomes distant and secretive.

A real touch of wit comes from one of the earliest sequences when Kevin McCarthy makes a cameo as a fleeing madman chased by a mob who is almost run over by Bennell. This forms a resonant connection to the first film that is picked up later at certain other opportune points, like the play on the Siegel version when Becky screams at the sight of a dog in danger, thus showing emotion and exposing herself as an unsnatched human. Here, Brooke Adams again screams at the sight of a dog, and what a creature it is—a mutant, vagrant-faced canine created by a faulty pod. Rather than take himself completely seriously as either a horror aficionado or a social satirist, Kaufman ably tinkered with the film to poke fun at New Age clap-trap that was all the rage in San Francisco at the time. No longer are we given to underpinnings of communism or government entanglement, but instead are held up to witness our own foibles and absurdity and held accountable for mind-numbing conformity.

Here too is the introduction of "the screech," that horrifying inhuman sound that pod people make to alert their fellow pods that a human still walks among them. This singular special sound effect—with face contorted into a leering mask, finger outstretched and pointed in accusation, with that hideous noise prevailing—makes for the most powerful ending of any film version. As Matthew and Elizabeth reach the well-guarded fields, again our heroine falls prey to exhaustion, and her body literally turns to dust in Matthew's arms as he sobs uncontrollably and watches in complete horror as she collapses and disintegrates.

It's also notable that this is the only version where our hero eventually loses his identity, becomes changed over, and follows his love to emotionless pod-dom. (If the lovers are reunited may this, in fact, be a sort of contented conclusion?) This allows for the awful and memorable last moment of the film where Matthew is approached by Veronica Cartwright—a friend previously thought to have been "snatched" but who's somehow managed to escape—and leaves us with the haunting image of Matthew in full screech, pointing her out with that ghastly noise arising, calling forth his pod brethren.

Transposing political viewpoints from the original film, where the police and military promise to eradicate the alien infestation, Abel Ferrara's *Body Snatchers* takes place on a military base itself, the microcosms shifting full circle. No longer is the United States government our ultimate benefactor and savior of freedom and generations to come—now the infestation ironically *begins* with those who are to be our protectors.

For this 1993 effort we have the dutiful Environment Protection Agency official and his family encountering the pods in a southern military base. The fact that the setting is so isolated—shades of the secluded Mill Valley—is both a help and a hindrance to the ambiance generated. We're not given to the worldwide panic or nationwide (or at least citywide) frenzy, yet the detached environment shows us the step by step assimilation, imperturbable and coldly logical, the pods like the soldiers themselves performing their duty for God and country.

However, the concept of alienated teen is used to great benefit. After being put through paranoia hell—put so succinctly by Meg Tilly as the overtaken, creepy mother figure with terrifying clear enunciation: "Where you gonna go, where you gonna hide, when there's nobody... left... like you?"—Gabrielle Anwar as the feisty daughter, and her soldier-protector boyfriend, steal a helicopter and blow up the base and trucks leaving for all around the country. The chopper lands at an airport in Atlanta, which may or may not be crawling with more of our favorite pod people.

While the ultimate fate of humanity is left "up in the air" (pun fully intended), one more modern Hollywood element that Abel Ferrara put into his film is the introduction of high firepowered vengeance. We may be having our world overrun by alien plant life, but that doesn't mean we have to sit back and take it lightly. No small gas fires set in

distant fields here; we haven't been inflating that defense
budget for nothing. Ferrara relishes in showing missile
after missile blasting pods, convoys of trucks, and all inter-
loping aliens to kingdom come. This gratuitous violence at
this point—a cathartic moment for everyone who wanted
to see the malefactors get at least a part of their comeup-
pance—undermined the pure horrific nature of being
powerless. Still, Ferrara's vision is updated enough for us to
feel the shifting tide of the nineties era, from terrorized,
cringing helplessness to a take-charge, take arms, Hollywood action mindset.

Though the novel *The Body Snatchers*—in all three of its
forms, including its original serialization in *Collier's* magazine—and the following three movie adaptations are all
certainly products of their eras and American cultural
influences, the thread weaving through all variations of
this story is one that is especially ironic and biting con-
cerning the subject matter at hand: what it means to be
human.

INVASION OF THE SCENE STEALERS: MY SECOND CAREER AS A GENRE ICON

— — —

by Kevin McCarthy
as told to Matthew R. Bradley
Research Associate: Gilbert Colon

Beginning with the so-called "Film School Generation" of directors (e.g., Steven Spielberg, George Lucas), latter-day genre filmmakers have shown their affection for the beloved sci-fi films of the '50s in various ways, from outright remakes to homages, and one of the most notable is in their use of instantly recognizable genre icons from that era. In the half-century or so since *Invasion of the Body Snatchers* (1956) was filmed, Kevin McCarthy has been cast in a number of roles not only because he is a diverse and talented actor, but also because he *is* Kevin McCarthy, the star of the classic Don Siegel original, who despite his long and distinguished résumé remains best known as Dr. Miles Bennell. We asked McCarthy (whose energy and enthusiasm belie his impressive age of ninety-one) to reflect on this secondary phase of his career, working with the likes of Joe Dante, Robert Rodriguez, Philip Kaufman, and even

Kevin McCarthy

"Weird Al" Yankovic in roles that ranged in spirit from serious to silly, and in size from quick cameos to full-fledged "leads."

Matthew R. Bradley: When did you learn about director Philip Kaufman's plan to create a new version of *Invasion of the Body Snatchers* (1978), and how did you happen to appear in it?

Kevin McCarthy: Okay; imagine me in the '70s, a good twenty years beyond '56, still trying to hustle acting jobs, hoping to land some kind of interesting assignment in whatever films were being cast. Not drek material, of course, but I guess I had the conceited idea I could find unusual acting opportunities in roles often thought to be hopeless. Divorce had come to pass after twenty years of trying for smooth sailing, so I had to get out of the house I felt at home in—and find a way to start a new life. Scary. A precarious existence, but what the hell, the woods're full of divorced guys like me sweating out the cost of child support, et cetera. Trying to see my three kids got college educations kept me focused; looking relentlessly for profitable employment on Stage, Screen, Television… Burlesque.

Anyway, summer of 1977 found me scrounging around, looking for work at Metro-Goldwyn-Mayer in Culver City, CA. Specifically, I was trying to track down a producer, James B. Harris, who'd been an early partner of the illustrious director Stanley Kubrick, before that man had achieved renown with his astonishing cinematic gifts. Rumor had it that Mr. Harris had taken an office on the MGM lot, and quite possibly had a fascinating film-project up his sleeve.

By God! Curiously enough, it's just now become clear to me, even as we're chatting: Stanley Kubrick is the answer to your query of how I came to be in *Body Snatchers II.*

Bradley: How so?

McCarthy: 1948, New York City. Montgomery Clift, my wife, Augusta Dabney, and I had been great old pals from the day we met back in 1942. We'd acted together in a play, *Mexican Mural,* which "Gadge" Kazan and Bobby Lewis (Group Theatre veterans) were trying out. Turned out to be an unsuccessful scheme to start a "Dollar-Top Theatre" on Broadway. Five years or so later, Montgomery Clift's career had taken off; he'd become a film star of unparalleled fame following the release of *Red River* [1948], the huge hit film he'd made with John Wayne. Next, Monty was partnered with Elizabeth Taylor in George Stevens' new picture, *A Place in the Sun* [1951]—another sensation. My buddy was suddenly besieged by hordes of public relations mavens, photographers, press agents, et cetera. To avoid stiff, posed photo set-ups, Clift insisted on some "activity" he could get involved in, to help mitigate his self-consciousness. Well, on this particular day, *McCarthy family-life* became the "activity."

Look magazine, a popular pictorial periodical—a rival of *Life*—had proposed that our pal do an extensive segment for them, "Montgomery Clift: Among Friends." Monty accepted. So, the wife and I and our little not yet two-year-old son, "Flip," and Monty horsed around for the camera.

We'd been waiting for the *Look* camera-team on the garden walkway outside our Peter Cooper Village apartment-house, on East River Drive in Manhattan. Well, *Look* magazine's "lens-team" turned out to be one solitary, hardly full-grown photographer with a camera case dangling from his neck, gliding toward us on roller skates! *Look* magazine had sent a child to shoot a photo-spread of Monty the movie star? "I'm Stanley Kubrick," he said. "Now why don't you stand over here…"

"No! No!" Monty said quickly. Various passers-by were becoming aware of the glamorous film star and it embarrassed him. "No, let's get ourselves into the elevator and do our thing up in '4-G,'" which was the McCarthys' ramshackle three-and-a-half-room palace. Monty had an easy, natural charm—he grabbed the roller skates and said, "Let me tote your wheels, Stanley." The shoot in our flat was easy and fun. Kubrick, young as he was, seemed adept and efficient. *Look* used several very good shots from that session and a batch more in some movie "mag" they also published. The 22-year-old

Kubrick was amiable and at ease during his assignment. Our lively initial encounter flowered over the next few months into a flock of get-togethers with young Kubrick. He'd phone and invite us to join him at one or another small Times Square screening room. His lively enthusiasm was contagious as he hopped around showing us the product of a number of basic photographic experiments he'd been working on—with certain lenses, I guess, and, I think, a simple 16 mm. motion-picture camera. Imagine Stanley, clearly pleased with what he was finding, projecting his pictorial discoveries onto a tiny screen for our viewing pleasure! I vividly recall seeing a brief scene he had shot by the light of flickering candles, later used so effectively in *Barry Lyndon* [1975]. To think now, that we saw the very first moments of his incredible career. Mind-boggling.

Bradley: You ever include this tidbit of an autobiographical anecdote in any previous "inquisition?"

McCarthy: No, dammit! Slipped my mind. That summer's day, at Metro in '77, was nigh onto thirty years after my acquaintance with Kubrick. Knowing, as I did, of Jim Harris' early association with Stanley, one can easily dope out why I had a hunch Jamie might have a film-story he hoped to produce. But when I located him he was totally mum about his film plans; all he really had to say to me was, "Did you know Don Siegel is on the lot?"

"Hell no!," cried I. "Where can I find the guy?"

Well, Jamie volunteered to walk me over to Don's office and kindly did so. Evidently Siegel was busy with last-minute editing on his forthcoming work, *Telefon* [1977], with Charles Bronson, Lee Remick, and Tyne Daly. But when he caught sight of me in his office, a characteristic yelp pierced the air. "Kiddo!" he bellowed, his face twisted in a friendly sardonic smile. In a trice we are exchanging hearty hugs. Next moment, Siegel begins to question me on my propitious timing. "How d'ja know?" he asked. "Who let the cat out of the bag?"

I'm mystified. "What cat? What bag? What's up, pal?"

Siegel's reply: "*The Body Snatchers* are 'up,' and I shall be one of 'em. Good timing!" He then spilled the beans about a secret new version of our famous 1956 film, which, he said, was in the works. "Right now! Right here on the MGM lot, 100 feet down the street! Phil Kaufman's directing. A screenwriter gent, by name W.D. Richter, has fashioned a contemporary script, but 'Pods' will still be pervading the action. Oh, yes! Heavy-duty plans exist to scare the hell out of everybody again. But this time not the dorky inhabitants of a tank town like Santa Mira. Huh-uh, San

Francisco's going to be the deadly venue for *Invasion of the Body Snatchers II!*"

Just for the fun of it, Kaufman had talked Siegel into making an uncredited, freebie appearance in the film as a "Pod" cab-driver and, says Don, "I bet he'd also love to have the leading man! Let's go over to his cage right now, and see if he doesn't fall for you."

And, by Jove, he did! I met the youngish Phil Kaufman and liked him right off. "Kevin," he inquired immediately, "would you be willing to do a couple of words, or, you know, some little 'shtick' that we might slip into our picture-show?"

"Absolutely!" says I. So, bingo! I'd committed myself. No doubt, all hands were in the dark about what the McCarthy cameo might be. As was I.

Oddly, nary a word did I hear from the producer of *Snatchers II*. Robert H. Solo was that obscure being who never touched base with me—no word or call about a contract, no work-dates or travel arrangements. I began to wonder if *"Pod Piece II"* only existed in Kaufman's imagination. So I hied myself back East, where life for me had a lot more texture than in La-La Land.

I admit I was disappointed about the cameo but eventually thoughts of Kaufman's *Body Snatchers II* disappeared into my mental waste-disposal system. Then I learned that Phil was shooting in San Francisco, with a strong cast headed by Donald Sutherland, Brooke Adams, Leonard Nimoy, and Jeff Goldblum. I was more disappointed, until my phone rang: my presence was required—on the set—immediately. I should proceed directly from the airport to the location site where the company would be rehearsing. Well, I was damn miffed about having to languish in limbo for so long, so I considered sulking on the East Coast. But curiosity was too much. Landing in the Bay area, I tracked straight to the location—which turned out to be a sleazy area of San Francisco's backside known as Skid Row. Not a place for a picnic.

The First A.D. [assistant director] on the film clarified my situation: "Second A.D.'ll bring you to your dressing room. You'll find the shooting-schedule, your script pages, wardrobe…and you are just in time for lunch! Everyone's looking forward to meeting you, and Mr. Kaufman's rarin' to go."

"Well, first, somebody must have a contract for me to sign—it never reached me in the Big Apple."

"Uh, that's Solo's department, Mr. McCarthy."

"Call me 'Kevin.'"

"Nah! You're 'Biff' to me!" he said, referring to my Oscar-nominated role in *Death of a Salesman* [1951]. Except for an "Obie" I won many years later, that's the only award I ever got close to. Anyway, I get to the dressing-trailer, curious to see what my cameo was, and find—a single phrase identifying it: *"Pods" chase Mr. McCarthy (Don't shave!)*. What in hell...?

A knock on my trailer dressing-room door and a voice calling, "It's Robert Solo! May I come in?" The Producer—the man with the dough!

Bradley: I'd guess your appearance in the picture was to be gratis.

McCarthy: You're reading ahead. Yes! There'd be no contract. Solo kept rattling on, "No, no, no! No contract! Kevin, you're doing this voluntarily, remember? Phil asked you and you said, 'Yes, sure!,' like Mr. Siegel's doing. Uncredited and uncompensated... like a contribution... like you're wishing us well. You won't be sorry; Phil has a fabulous scene you'll be doing with, uh, uh, Donald Sutherland! I can't wait to see what you come up with!"

I think Solo eventually gave me some pocket-money, maybe 100 bucks. Do you wonder that I felt twinges of resentment when I was hard up, grousing to myself about those several thousands of dollars of residuals I'd never see?

Bradley: Did Solo call your attention to Robert Duvall's unexplained presence in the movie? The guy is simply sitting there swinging in a swing, also uncredited and unpaid, perhaps.

McCarthy: Hmnn, I never doped out Duvall's appearance in the show, unless they had him in there representing the "swingers" of Skid Row.

Bradley: Are you now saying you regret doing the cameo in Phil's Kaufman's movie? Brief as the scene is, don't you feel it stands up as a strong episode in the proceedings?

McCarthy: I'm saying we ought to suppress the term *cameo*! It's far more—an *Episode*—a bloody goddam *Scene*—whatever! Yeah, and an intrinsic element in the picture! Right here's where the "Pods" will be coming into sight chasing old Doc Bennell, twenty years later and "still on the job." Phil's cameras'll take in the whole mess, this grungy Skid Row intersection. The film company, for crisakes, has got the area rife with all kinds of human flotsam—drab-looking pedestrians (SAG extras), a motley assortment of beat-up cars, choking the streets, motors idlin', horns blarin', Sutherland's car is there, stunt drivers waiting for Kaufman to shout "Action!" when the traffic signal changes. Phil Kaufman gives me a warm greeting and starts talking me through the scene: "It's nearly twenty-five years since Miles Bennell had brought the 'Pod Plague' to an end, but our idea, Kevin, is that—mysteriously and terrifyingly—those deadly objects have reappeared! Here! Yes! Right here—in San Francisco! All around town! And now, in your cameo, Kevin, we behold an incredible sight:

you! Dr. Bennell, a frantic figure, appearing here at this crowded intersection, on the run from a vicious gang of those accursed, soulless beings. Yes! The apogee of horror is their gift to our humanity! But now, you, Miles, get a glimpse of the Health Service logo on Sutherland's car, stopped by the light—only a step or two away! *You fling yourself onto the hood! Scream your warning to the occupants: 'Listen to me! Listen!' Fists battering the cracked windshield, you shriek your warning again to the driver! 'They're coming!' You leap from the hood to seize the driver's side car-door handle! Keerist! Too late! The driver instantly locks it! 'NO! NO!' Oh God! The chasing goons see you! You must not be caught!* Around the corner—there's *a chance to get away! Take it!* Then I'll call cut! Of course, around that fateful corner, we will see grisly evidence that a hit-and-run 'Pod-Mobile' has smashed Dr. Miles to smithereens. We'll need one scary shot of you 'kaput!' Okay? *A battered slab of bloody pulp, face-down in the Skid Row muck.* I'll grab that shot later," Phil assures me. Great!

Bradley: You don't think Kaufman dumped a bit too much on your plate?

McCarthy: All in a day's work, pal. The irony of this situation with Phil is that this so-called cameo is a major event wherein my character, Dr. Miles Bennell (a human archangel-like Jeremiah), is reprising the most vital scene of the original film in a kind of whimsical, and somewhat joking, way. And I'm feeling pretty stupid about it now. Feels as though Kaufman's gag made me an inadvertent accomplice of the "Pods!" Yet there I was, with little concern, trifling with our legendary achievement—damn near demolishing it when we're confronted with the gruesome and fatal *rubbing out* of me, the good doctor, in the vile Skid Row muck!

Ah! The spineless actor, so carried away with the opportunity to be "doing his stuff," he goes trampling in picturesque fashion over anything and everything. Showing off! Uncredited and unpaid. What a guy! Oy gevalt!

Bradley: Do you think Kaufman's version, with its '70s sensibility, was warning us about different dangers than those of the original picture? The big-city setting suggests so to me; yet the fact that you are still running after twenty-odd years may mean nothing has changed.

McCarthy: C'mon, something that significant was in anyone's skull as those spooky moments on Skid Row were being put on film? No doubt there are unusual, powerful, off-the-wall psyches that pleasure themselves dickering with ambiguous questions like that. Me, I'm unable to spend time looking into all the hypothetical alternatives between A and B. I recall seeing Phil's film at its premiere in Manhattan and was entertained by it—lots of spectacular wild and colorful sci-fi features throughout. Yet finally I have to say

Body Snatchers II, for me, doesn't hold a candle to the potent dynamics of what Don Siegel had wrought, twenty years earlier, in glorious black and white.

Bradley: Personally, I admire the film quite a bit, although the original remains untouched.

McCarthy: That's showbiz. But a strikingly effective factor in producer Walter Wanger's original *Body Snatchers* is how plain and unembellished nearly all the settings were. How little you see! The grotesque elements are used very sparingly, not splayed all over the screen. For Siegel, the viewer's *imagination* is the scene-shop and the viewer's *mind* is the fearful chamber wherein grim and grisly events're being experienced. We players, in our actions and doings, are suggesting certain dire possibilities, while you in your psyches fill out the dread dimensions.

Bradley: On the subject of interpretations, many have asserted that Siegel's film was attacking McCarthyism, based on the notorious Senator Joseph McCarthy and his anticommunist diatribes. I have read that you are unrelated to "Tailgunner Joe," but that you and Senator Eugene McCarthy, a Democrat from Minnesota, are kindred.

McCarthy: Not related to either, and fortunately, the good "Gene" McC. was an altogether different cup of tea, the antithesis of the slandering villain from the neighboring state of Wisconsin, though by chance Gene and I do bump into each other occasionally. His higher education occurred at a Benedictine monastery, St. John's University, in Collegeville, Minnesota, about eight miles north of where, oddly enough, his young non-relative, Kevin, was attending St. Benedict's High School and College. This was a sizeable Catholic boarding school for girls located in the one-horse town of St. Joe, Minnesota. Inclusive of a couple of platoons of nuns, who were faculty, some two hundred females were ensconced in various dorms, or more up-scale housing arrangements. St. Ben's was, and maybe still is, a substantial collection of imposing Romanesque structures sitting on well cared-for grounds and gardens in the rural countryside. A Boy's School existed (for boy boarders only—no "day-dogs!"). Thirty-five or forty boys of elementary-school age comprised our studentbody. Sitting slightly apart from the rather classier venues serving the feminine population, the Boys-School abode was a lackluster ancient red brick building, combining dorm facilities and a couple of classrooms. Us little guys were well away from, but not unaware of, all those mysterious young female beings. The Benedictine nuns, our guardians and teachers, were mysterious, too, but one got used to them. Luckily, I made it through eighth grade somehow and was out and away from that welter of femininity before puberty had me in its fascinating clutches. And a good thing, too.

Bradley: Did you and "Gene McC." ever talk about the film?

McCarthy: I doubt it. I met him, voted for him and enjoyed his company. Enough. Period.

Bradley: According to *Leonard Maltin's Movie Guide*, the original version of producer Wanger's *Body Snatchers* movie was reissued, in 1979, without the studio-imposed prologue and epilogue. Have you seen this 76-minute de facto director's cut, and if so, do you prefer it to the studio's version?

McCarthy: Reissued by whom? Smells fishy to me. Of course it's intriguing to consider I may be the last to know of it. Never saw it. Never heard about it, until I checked you out, Matthew! I did find a line or two about it in *Maltin's Almanac.* To me it's all baloney. How can the narration be erased from the sound-track without disastrous damage? Could be some nutty amateur effort, I suppose. Next time I catch sight of Leonard out here, I'm sure as hell going to get the scoop on it. Don Siegel fought fiercely for his original "direc-tor's cut" but finally had to admit, "Kevin, my friend, the 'Pods' beat us. We have to live with that." Maybe in these fearful days that we're sweating out in the U.S. of A., Latter-Day "Pods" are infiltrating our society in a dangerous way. Or somehow, from afar, beyond the solar system and the black holes, those soulless organic beings are even now taking a cosmic swat at us!

Bradley: How did your long and fruitful collaboration with director Joe Dante come about?

McCarthy: *Piranha* [1978], his first picture [as a solo director]. I remember he said, "The money's no good, but what about doing it anyway? I'll only need you for, maybe a couple days, up in Griffith Park, and down in Austin, Texas, for a week. We'll do the rest of your deeds in and around the lake down there." Somehow he found some money, and I did the job, and I've never regretted it. Despite a modest host of negative qualities he can be a terrific fellow and a neat person altogether. He approaches whatever he's up to with a lighthearted ardor. He's stuck with a valuable sense of humor and a sardonic nature. Siegel also had that sardonical element in his make-up. I don't know what to make of that "symbiosis."

Bradley: Dante and John Sayles, who had written *Piranha*, turned *The Howling* (1981) into the ultimate "in-joke" by not only casting icons from a variety of genres (e.g., Patrick Macnee, Slim Pickens), but also naming most of the characters after directors of previous werewolf films. Did you share a chuckle with the real-life "Fred Francis" over that when you appeared in his ill-fated *Dark Tower* (1987)?

McCarthy: I try to avoid sharing chuckles. But I suspect I wasn't aware of Joe's blip of humor during those grisly, hopelessly conceived scenes in Barcelona that Fred had to work on. Despite the difficulties, he was clearly a talented, gracious, and attractive person.

Bradley: I understand he had his name taken off the movie and a pseudonym put on instead.

McCarthy: A reasonable act.

Bradley: In Dante's section of *Twilight Zone—The Movie* (1983), you ad-libbed a reference to your classic 1960 episode from the first season of Rod Serling's *Twilight Zone* series, "Long Live Walter Jameson."

McCarthy: [sourly] That impromptu line didn't make it into the finished film. [At this point, Kevin stands and becomes the Uncle Walt character.] "When ah headed over ta mah favorite beat-up ol' armchair, ta await da bash-outta-existence the kid's a'gonna deal me, an' ah was jes' a'plumpin' m'self down onto its comfy stash'o crud an' ol' comic books, guess what? Jes' as ah'm settlin' ma 'keister' down, it cum inta contack with somethin' lumpy under them cushions. Wal, what ah yanked out from them pillas was a corked-up ol' medicine bottle still holdin' a coupl'a swallas a' ol' corn likker! Heh! Lak a bat outta hell ah'd chawed that cork out, an'—figgerin' ah was a 'goner' anyway—ah raised that 'crock-'a booze' 'n' toasted mahself with a snort: 'Lordy, it sher looks lak it's curtains fer "everlastin'"' Walt Jameson!'"

Lights all begin flashing wildly, signifying the kid was blowing me to kingdom come. Kingdom "gone" is what happened. That shot ain't in the movie! Dante blamed the lab for screwin' things up. Some dern thing sure put the fritz on what ah hoped'd be a Jim Dandy, kick-ass, whiz-bang exit.

Bradley: Have you made other appearances relating to *The Twilight Zone?*

McCarthy: Hard to say, man. My life's a *Twilight Zone*— I'm ninety-one years old.

Bradley: While Dante did not cast you in *Gremlins* (1984), he did show a scene from *Invasion of the Body Snatchers* playing on TV. He also surprised you with a giant seed pod on the set of *InnerSpace* (1987), had Christopher Lee carrying one in *Gremlins 2: The New Batch* (1990), and cast you as "Dr. Bennell" in *Looney Tunes: Back in Action* (2003). What do you think makes him—and others—keep coming back to *The Body Snatchers?*

McCarthy: It's a classic—it'll be inscribed on my tombstone.

Bradley: *UHF* (1989) is a virtual catalog of pop-culture references, incorporating the music videos of "Weird Al" Yankovic. How did you get involved in this offbeat film?

McCarthy: Don't quite recall how it came to pass but I'm certainly damn glad it did. Somebody got my telephone number, I suppose, an' I got a call from a Jay Levey [the director] saying he and Mr. Yankovic wished to discuss a film idea. They wanted to know if I could meet them at a most unpretentious café, some-

Kevin McCarthy

where in a part of town I'd never been. So I found my way there, and we sat around for an hour or so. I was only vaguely aware of Mr. Yankovic's act: taking popular songs and re-doing the lyrics with sardonic commentary, while accompanying himself on the accordion. Funny guy.

So Al, a nice fellow with a unique talent, and Jay, a modest spirit, and I, an ordinary citizen, just sat there schmoozing.

At long last Jay said to me, "You know what we really have in mind? We want to find somebody who's willing to play the meanest man who ever lived."

"You have come to the appropriate guy," I replied, and kicked him in the shin to prove it. "That's me! Me! Oh, yes! Me! Here I am! Where do we put the camera?" And that's how I got the job. I'm quite adept at behaving mean and nasty in real life, and was thrilled to imagine this slick talent of mine magnified to fill CINERAMA'S WIDEST SCREENS.

Despicable rottenness delivered with a little subtlety does indeed intrigue me as a performer. I recall during filming of *UHF* doing a couple of scenes for those bozos—playing Weird Al's boss, Fletcher, a quality creep, and making him, I'm sure, as vile as could be.

"Cut!" calls Levey. "Make him meaner, will you? C'mon Kevin, more of the real you, old boy!"

So much for subtlety.

Bradley: I gather, then, that you enjoy the opportunities such roles offer for larger-than-life performances, which can help make a brief appearance so memorable?

McCarthy: Yeah, acting sure as hell is an "on the nose" profession for me. I'm not keen, however, at finding myself on screen in less-than-electrifying Brief Encounters. Yet now, as I begin to mature, I must admit rich roles rarely come my way anymore…

Bradley: After more than fifty years, I'd say you've made very much the best of it.

McCarthy: Oh, Bosh. Put that in caps.

Bradley: Dante's *Matinee* (1993) paid tribute to legendary showman William Castle. Did you feel that its film-within-a-film, *Mant*, properly captured that '50s sci-fi spirit?

McCarthy: Never paid much attention to opinions pro or con about films, other than the picture-shows I've been in. I'm aware there are people, even some critics, who're genuine students of film, and they write about them—and write philosophical tomes at times. I can say, however, that Richard Schickel's work appeals to me. Now, you, Matthew R., partnered here with "K.," this 190 pounds of thespic margarine—you know a lot, I'm told, about what's been done. I'm also told people hold you in high regard. Good! I'm happy to be learning from you as we eke our way through this curious enterprise. I'm sure you've noted I'm an unsophisticated student of genres in film. The dimly-lit "opinion-closet" in my head sees little action. Only a modicum of particular convictions've stuck around for long...

Bradley: Dante often makes similar use of your fellow icons like Dick Miller, William Schallert, Kenneth Tobey, and director Roger Corman. Do you consider yourselves a kind of unofficial "stock company," and do you guys hang out together at conventions?

McCarthy: I've broken bread with Joe, but I try to steer clear of the competition, even though they're apparently decent citizens, probably fine pillars of humanity. When I see Schallert, I think, "That guy's working again, and I'm not—Hell's bells!" Actually, when *Twilight Zone—The Movie* was made, Joe sent me a scene from the screenplay, suggesting I could play the father. But I caught sight of a really gooney uncle in the family—a chance for some gags and horseplay. I suggested to Joe that I'd prefer that role rather than the dad. Dante, no doubt, checked with Spielberg, who was producing and, in the end, Bill Schallert did the dad.

I could hardly wait to play that rumpusly funny, strange, weird old bird, the uncle, and I saw a lot of opportunities to run a little wild.

Joe said, "Well, you sure as hell are running

wild in the screening room, Kevin!"

"You're going to use it, aren't you, Joe? Some of it? Any of it?"

"Well, it's questionable, Mr. McCarthy, how much we can use of you and your 'off the wall' capers. But at least you're having a hell of a go in the dailies!"

Uncle Walt's great fun to watch, and I had fun. Schallert, an accomplished actor, was a tiptop father figure, plus he's a past President of our Guild, so he must be respected. Or not [laughs].

Bradley: Were you approached about Abel Ferrara's *Body Snatchers* (1993)?

McCarthy: Nope.

Bradley: What was your opinion of Jack Finney's original novel, *The Body Snatchers?*

McCarthy: Before coming out to California to do the picture, back in '55, Don Siegel called to tell me the piece, entitled *The Body Snatchers,* was being serialized in *Collier's,* a weekly magazine. Walter Wanger had acquired the rights. Siegel knew me pretty well—my vigor, my vitality…my vanity—from our work together in *An Annapolis Story,* a film he directed in '54. I was delighted Don wanted me for the male lead in his new venture.

But in no way could I even begin to imagine it on the screen. How in hell did Don expect to make that weird story? And, of course,

Dan Mainwaring's screenplay didn't come anywhere near much of what's in the novel. That's okay; whatever's there in his screenplay certainly did the job. I'd like to see somebody try to do the novel—as written.

Bradley: Your sister, Mary, was a novelist. I wondered if she had an opinion regarding Jack Finney and his *Body Snatchers*, or was a reader of sci-fi literature at all?

McCarthy: No, she wasn't; I doubt she knew Finney's name. Mary was a singularly gifted writer, one of the finest stylists in the English language. Hardly a week goes by that I don't see her name in print, quoted as an authority on one thing or another.

There's a unique, very interesting volume, *Seeing Mary Plain: A Life of Mary McCarthy*, by Frances Kiernan, who was a pillar on the *New Yorker* editorial staff. Her book, tantalizing, amusing, rare, creative, feisty, is composed of manifold interviews—150 or so of 'em—with people who either were very involved with Mary and admired her enormously, or took issue with her work or her position on certain subjects—literary, political, social, or whatever—and detested her. "Her pen is dipped in vitriol!," some said. Read any two or three sentences of Mary's work and you'll derive infinite pleasure, just in the way she couches her words and phrases. Her mind was marvelous, and her humor exquisite, though a lot of people don't get it. It's a little too oblique or laid-

back. But if you ever heard her read—on
stage at the 92nd Street YMHA in New
York, for instance, you'd find the audience
enjoying the humor that emerged from her
phrasing; choruses of delighted laughter
always embellished her evenings.

Bradley: In the Robert Rodriguez film *Roadracers*
(1994), you are seen sitting in a theater as
"Miles," discussing the meaning of *The Body
Snatchers* with a viewer, a role that I assume
you've frequently played in real life. What's
your stock answer, if any, regarding the
film's McCarthy-era message, and the irony
of your last name?

McCarthy: If I detect an insinuation in your query that
I deal or have dealt in "stock" answers,
Matthew, you are grievously mistaken. The
truth is, never did I see or hear, during the
course of the filming, anything about Joe
McCarthy or McCarthyism. No question, lots
of people saw our picture as a political allegory, believing that's what we who gave life
to the story had intended. The only conclusion I reached, when wondering what
author Finney had in mind while writing
The Body Snatchers, was that he was trying to
shed light on the idea that embracing "conformity," as a way of life, could lead to the
kind of society that gave us the Nazis.

Conformity. Lew Wasserman, powerhouse
chief of Music Corporation of America
[MCA], a talent agency that bought Universal Studios, insisted on sartorial conformity

from his minions at his palatial offices in Beverly Hills. Lew affected somber, funereal attire: black suits, white shirts, blue or black ties. His employees affected identical garb. Except some of the ladies. Can you, Matthew, picture that? Can you imagine what that conformity might have spawned?!

Bradley: So, if Siegel, screenwriter Daniel Mainwaring, or any other members of the cast and crew had anything else on their minds, they didn't tell you about it, right?

McCarthy: Well, I think I certainly knew what was going on with Siegel all the way through. He loathed the *Invasion of the Body Snatchers* title. Dumbos at Allied Artists discovered that the *Collier's* serial title was also the name of a Robert Louis Stevenson work. Author Jack Finney used it for his story in *Collier's*, but—oops!—some alert underling at Allied Artists awoke on April Fool's Day 1955 to the fact that ten years previously a movie called *The Body Snatcher* was made [from Stevenson's story]. And it starred those two great horror figures, Boris Karloff and Bela Lugosi! Worse news: that movie was still in release. Meanwhile, Siegel's players, unaware of titular adversities, were shooting what is often characterized as the all-time classic *sci-fi* motion picture. In any event, we damn well could not have two *Body Snatcher* films going head to head, toe to toe, cheek to cheek, hip to thigh—stuff like that...

Bradley: Okay, Kev, we've got it!

McCarthy: What was to be done? Well, the industry knew that flocks of spooky, cheap, weird, sci-fi-ish exploitation flicks were out there at the time: *Invaders from Mars* [1953], *Freaks from Outer Space.* Stuff like that was infesting the country's drive-ins and making much moolah. Well, some genius, at Allied Artists' Sunset Studios in Hollywood, came up with the notion of linking an exploitative term that implied "space" terror—*Invasion of*—to *The Body Snatchers.* Eureka!

               The rest is history. Don Siegel called Wanger a "Pod" for letting the studio use that title. But as Kurt Vonnegut would say, "So it goes!" I came up with the title Siegel preferred: *Sleep No More!* It's from *Hamlet* [as well as *Macbeth*]. We were overruled.

Bradley: You joined Dick Miller and Schallert in Dante's *The Second Civil War* (1997), where an immigration issue sparks a Constitutional crisis. Are you a fan of "poli-sci-fi"?

McCarthy: I'm a fan of Joe Dante's. Whenever he's doing anything, I'm going to be there, if he can use me. Hell, no big deal. You expect the work is going to be mostly interesting and there'll be good times along the way.

Bradley: Any other *Body Snatchers*-related appearances we've missed?

McCarthy: No, sir. This jig is up, pardner. Thank you, M.R.!

Bradley: Well, I'll be ridin' off into the sunset, if you're lookin' for me.

McCarthy: How about that fella!

KEVIN McCARTHY FILMOGRAPHY

2003 Looney Tunes: Back in Action

1998 Addams Family Reunion

1995 Just Cause

1995 Liz: the Elizabeth Taylor Story

1995 Steal Big, Steal Little

1994 Roadracers

1994 Judicial Consent

1994 Greedy

1992 Duplicates

1992 Tales From the Crypt: Curiosity Killed

1992 Matinee

1992 The Distinguished Gentleman

1991 Final Approach

1991 Dead on the Money

1991 Ghoulies III: Ghoulies Go to College

1990 Eve of Destruction

1990 The Sleeping Car

1990 The Rose and the Jackal

1989 Fast Food

1989 Passion and Paradise, Part 1

1989 UHF

1989 Passion and Paradise, Part 2

1988 Dark Tower

1988 Once Upon a Texas Train

1988 Love or Money?

1988 For Love or Money

1988 In the Heat of the Night

1987 Poor Little Rich Girl: The Barbara Hutton Story

1987 Hostage

1987 The Long Journey Home

1987 Innerspace

1986 A Masterpiece of Murder

1986 LBJ: The Early Years

1986 The Midnight Hour

1985 Deadly Intentions

1985 Murder, She Wrote: Armed Response

1984 Invitation to Hell

1984 The Mogul

1983 Making of a Male Model

1983 Twilight Zone: The Movie

1983 Montgomery Clift

1982 My Tutor

1982 Rosie: The Rosemary Clooney Story

1981 The Howling

1980 Flamingo Road

1980 Those Lips, Those Eyes

1980 Portrait of an Escort
1980 Hero at Large
1978 Piranha
1978 Invasion of the Body Snatchers
1977 Mary Jane Harper Cried Last Night
1977 The Exo-Man
1976 Aces High
1976 Buffalo Bill and the Indians, or Sitting Bull's History Lesson
1974 June Moon
1973 El Clan De Los Immorales
1973 Dan Candy's Law
1972 Kansas City Bomber
1972 A Great American Tragedy
1972 To Steal a King
1971 Mission: Impossible: Invasion
1969 U.M.C.
1969 The Last of the Powerseekers
1968 If He Hollers, Let Him Go
1968 Incident in Berlin
1968 Revenge at El Paso
1968 The Hell with Heroes
1967 Ace High
1967 Hotel

1966 A Big Hand for the Little Lady
1966 Mirage
1965 The Three Sisters
1964 The Alfred Hitchcock Hour: Beast in View
1964 An Affair of the Skin
1964 Fugitive, Vol. 3
1964 The Best Man
1963 The Prize
1963 A Gathering of Eagles
1963 40 Pounds of Trouble
1961 The Misfits
1960 The Twilight Zone: Long Live Walter Jameson
1958 Diamond Safari
1956 Invasion of the Body Snatchers
1956 Nightmare
1955 An Annapolis Story
1955 Stranger on Horseback
1954 Drive a Crooked Road
1954 The Gambler from Natchez
1952 Studio One: Jane Eyre
1951 Death of a Salesman
1944 Winged Victory

FILM CREDITS

1956

Invasion of the Body Snatchers Cast and Crew:

Kevin McCarthy (*Dr. Miles Bennel*)
Dana Wynter (*Becky Driscoll*)
Larry Gates (*Dr. Dan Kauffmann*)
King Donovan (*Jack*)
Carolyn Jones (*Theodore*)
Whit Bissell (*Dr. Hill*)
Jean Willes (*Sally*)
Ralph Dumke (*Nick*)
Tom Fadden (*Uncle Ira Lentz*)
Virginia Christine (*Wilma Lentz*)
Kenneth Patterson (*Driscoll*)
Guy Way (*Sam Janzek*)
Eileen Stevens (*Mrs. Grimaldi*)
Beatrice Maude (*Grandma*)
Jean Andren (*Aunt Eleda Lentz*)
Everett Glass (*Pursey*)
Dabbs Greer (*Mac*)
Pat O'Malley (*Man Carrying Baggage*)
Guy Rennie (*Proprietor*)
Richard Deacon (*Dr. Harvey Bassett*)
Harry Vejar (*With Man Carrying Baggage*)
Don Siegel
Bobby Clark (*Jimmy Grimaldi*)

Production Credits:

Jack Finney (*Book Author*)
Ellsworth Fredericks (*Cinematographer*)
Carmen Dragon (*Composer [Music Score]*)
Don Siegel (*Director*)
Robert S. Eisen (*Editor*)
Emile LaVigne (*Makeup*)
Walter Wanger (*Producer*)
Edward S. Haworth (*Production Designer*)
Joseph Kish (*Production Designer*)
Allen K. Wood (*Production Manager*)
Daniel Mainwaring (*Screenwriter*)
Joseph Kish (*Set Designer*)
Ralph Butler (*Sound/Sound Designer*)
Milt Rice (*Special Effects*)

1978

Invasion of the Body Snatchers Cast and Crew:

Donald Sutherland *(Matthew Bennell)*
Brooke Adams *(Elizabeth Driscoll)*
Leonard Nimoy *(Dr. David Kibner)*
Veronica Cartwright *(Nancy Bellicec)*
Jeff Goldblum *(Jack Bellicec)*
Art Hindle *(Geoffrey)*
Lelia Goldoni *(Katherine)*
Kevin McCarthy *(Running Man)*
Maurice Argent *(Chef)*
Joe Bellan *(Beggar)*
Tom Dahlgren *(Detective)*
Garry Goodrow *(Boccardo)*
Sam Hiona *(Policeman #1)*
Wood Moy *(Mr. Tong)*
Al Nalbandian *(Rodent Man)*
Jerry Walter *(Restaurant Owner)*
Robert Duvall *(Priest on Swing (uncredited))*
Jerry Garcia *(Banjo Player)*
Rose Kaufman *(Outraged Woman)*
Tom Luddy *(Ted Hendley)*
Don Siegel *(Taxi Driver)*

Production Credits:

Jack Finney *(Book Author)*
Mary Goldberg *(Casting)*
Michael Chapman *(Cinematographer)*
Denny Zeitlin *(Composer (Music Score))*
Philip Kaufman *(Director)*
Douglas Stewart *(Editor)*
Thomas R. Burman *(Makeup Special Effects)*
Edouard Henriques III *(Makeup Special Effects)*
Robert Solo *(Producer)*
Charles Rosen *(Production Designer)*
Alan Levine *(Production Manager)*
W.D. Richter *(Screenwriter)*
Doug von Koss *(Set Designer)*
Art Rochester *(Sound/Sound Designer)*
Russ Hessey *(Special Effects)*
Dell Rheaume *(Special Effects)*

1993

Body Snatchers Cast and Crew:
Gabrielle Anwar *(Marty Malone)*
Terry Kinney *(Steve Malone)*
Billy Wirth *(Tim Young)*
Meg Tilly *(Carol Malone)*
Forest Whitaker *(Major Collins)*
Christine Elise *(Genn Platt)*
R. Lee Ermey *(General Platt)*
Reilly Murphy *(Andy Malone)*
Kathleen Doyle *(Mrs. Platt)*
Tonea Stewart *(Teacher)*
Jennifer Tilly *(Body Double Meg)*
Phil Neilson *(MP Gate Captain)*
Keith Smith *(Soldier Gas Station)*
Ferne Cassel
Michael Cohen *(MP #5)*

Production Credits:
John Huke *(Art Director)*
Jack Finney *(Book Author)*
George Mooradian *(Camera Operator)*
Ferne Cassel *(Casting)*
Bojan Bazelli *(Cinematographer)*
Michael Jaffe *(Co-producer)*
Joe Delia *(Composer (Music Score))*
Margaret M. Mohr *(Costume Designer)*
Abel Ferrara *(Director)*
Anthony Redman *(Editor)*
Thomas R. Burman *(Makeup)*
Bari Dreiband-Burman *(Makeup)*
Robert Solo *(Producer)*
Peter Jamison *(Production Designer)*
Stuart Gordon *(Screenwriter)*
Dennis Paoli *(Screenwriter)*
Larry Cohen *(Screenwriter)*
Nicholas St. John *(Screenwriter)*
Linda Spheeris *(Set Designer)*
Raymond Cistheri *(Short Story Author)*
Phil Neilson *(Stunts)*

JACK FINNEY BIBLIOGRAPHY

5 Against the House (1954)

The Body Snatchers (1955, revised as
Invasion of the Body Snatchers, 1978)

Telephone Roulette: A Comedy in One Act (1956)

The House of Numbers (1957)

The Third Level (1957)
[pub in the UK as The Clock of Time, 1958]

Assault on a Queen (1959)

Good Neighbor Sam (1963)

I Love Galesburg in the Springtime (1963)

The Woodrow Wilson Dime (1968)

Time and Again (1970)

Marion's Wall (1973)

The Night People (1977)

Forgotten News: The Crime of the Century
and Other Lost Stories (1983)

From Time to Time (1995)